"Before you knew I was pregnant you didn't want me working for you. You said you don't want a PA. But it's clear you need one. So obviously there's a reason you're fighting having someone work for you."

He sighed.

"Fine. Don't tell me. Because I don't care. What I *do* care about is earning my keep."

He sighed again. "You are a pregnant woman who needs a rest. Just take the time here with me to have some fun."

She raised her chin. "No. If you won't let me work I won't take your charity. I'm going home."

"You don't have a home to go back to."

"Then let me stay here for two weeks as your assistant. If you don't like what I do, or still feel you don't need someone at the end of two weeks, I'll take another two weeks to rest and then go home."

When they'd first begun arguing, before he'd known she was pregnant, his eyes had been sharp. Glowing. She could have sworn he wanted to kiss her. It was as if he had been daring her to step closer—

Had he been daring her to step closer?

Dear Reader

I had such a wonderful time writing *Her Brooding Italian Boss*. Not only did I get to return to Italy, but I also took a little side trip to Spain! Boisterous, lovable billionaire Constanzo Bartulocci makes another appearance in this story about his son, Antonio, a painter who's lost his ability to create.

The heroine is Laura Beth Matthews, the final roommate of beautiful Olivia Prentiss and Eloise Vaughn. Because her roommates are stunning beauties, Laura Beth thinks she's an ugly duckling.

This story really resonated with me because I think this happens to a lot of us. We compare ourselves to others and wonder if we're lacking.

It takes a sacrifice on the part of both Antonio and Laura Beth—a little time when each has to step away from his or her own troubles—before they realise they might be the other's miracle.

And I love that too. LOL! Because that's really the bottom line to life. If you hurt, look around for someone who is hurting a bit more and be that person's miracle.

Happy reading!

Susan Meier

HER BROODING ITALIAN BOSS

BY
SUSAN MEIER

First published in Great Britain 2015
by Mills & Boon, an imprint of Harlequin (UK) Limited,
Eton House, 18-24 Paradise Road, Richmond, Surrey, TW9 1SR

© 2015 Linda Susan Meier

ISBN: 978-0-263-25740-3

Susan Meier is the author of over fifty books for Mills & Boon®. *The Tycoon's Secret Daughter* was a RITA® Finalist and *Nanny for the Millionaire's Twins* won the Book Buyers' Best award and was a finalist in the National Readers' Choice awards. She is married and has three children. One of eleven siblings, she loves to write about the complexity of families and totally believes in the power of love.

Books by Susan Meier

The Twelve Dates of Christmas
Daring to Trust the Boss
Single Dad's Christmas Miracle
Her Pregnancy Surprise
Kisses on Her Christmas List

Mothers in a Million

A Father for Her Triplets

The Larkville Legacy

The Billionaire's Baby SOS

First Time Dads!

Nanny for the Millionaire's Twins
The Tycoon's Secret Daughter

**Visit the author profile page at
www.millsandboon.co.uk for more titles**

CHAPTER ONE

LAURA BETH MATTHEWS sat on the rim of the old porcelain tub in the New York City apartment she had to vacate by the next morning. Her long brown hair had been swirled into a sophisticated French twist. Her lilac organza bridesmaid gown was an original Eloise Vaughn design. A pregnancy test shook in her right hand.

Tears pooled in her eyes. There was no question now. She was going to have a baby.

"Laura Beth! Come on!" Eloise called from the hall as she knocked on the bathroom door. "I'm the bride! I should at least get ten minutes in the bathroom to check my makeup."

"Sorry!" She swiped at her tears and quickly examined her face in the medicine cabinet mirror. No real mascara smudges yet, but the day was young.

For the first time since she, Eloise and their third original roommate, Olivia Prentiss Engle, had decided to spend the night before Eloise's wedding together and dress together, Laura Beth regretted it. She was pregnant. The father of her child, one of Olivia's husband's vice presidents, had called her a slut when she'd told him she was late and they might be parents. And now she didn't just have to smile her way through a wedding; she had to hide a pregnancy test in a tiny bathroom.

She glanced around. "I'll be two more seconds." Out of time, she wrapped the stick in toilet paper and tossed it in the little wastebasket. Satisfied neither Olivia nor Eloise would rummage through the trash, she sucked in a breath, pasted on a happy smile and opened the door.

Eloise stood before her, glowing, a vision in her original Artie Best gown, designed specifically by her boss, the one and only Artie Best. Smooth silk rode Eloise's feminine curves. Rhinestones sparkled across the sweetheart neckline. And real diamonds—enough to support the population of a third-world country for a decade—glittered at her throat.

Tears pooled in Laura Beth's eyes again, but this time they were tears of joy for her friend. Eloise, Olivia and Laura Beth had moved to New York City with stars in their eyes. Now Olivia was a married mom. Eloise would be married in a few hours. And Laura Beth was pregnant, with a deadbeat for her child's father and twenty-four hours to vacate her apartment.

She was in deep trouble.

Antonio Bartulocci studied his shoulder-length curly black hair in the mirror. He'd gotten it cut for Ricky and Eloise's wedding, but he still debated tying it back, out of the way. He looked to the left, then the right, and decided he was worrying over nothing. Eloise and Ricky were his friends because they liked him just as he was. They didn't care that he was a tad bohemian. Most artists were.

He straightened his silver tie one last time before he walked out of the bedroom of his suite in his father's Park Avenue penthouse and headed for the main room.

Comfortable aqua sofas faced each other atop a pale gray area rug, flanked by white Queen Anne chairs. A gray stone fireplace took up the back wall, and a dark walnut wet bar sat in the corner. The view of the New York City skyline from the wall of windows in the back had taken Antonio's breath away when he first saw it. Since his wife's death, it barely registered.

"Hurry up, Antonio," his father called from the bar as he poured bourbon into a crystal glass. He wore a simple black suit, a white shirt and yellow striped tie that would be replaced by a tuxedo for the reception later that night. Though he was well into his seventies and a few pounds overweight, Italian billionaire Constanzo Bartulocci was a dashing man. A man whose looks spoke of money and power, who lived not in an ordinary world, but in one he could control. Unlike Antonio's world, where passion, inspiration and luck ruled.

"I'm right behind you."

Constanzo jumped and faced his son, his right hand over his heart. "You scare me."

Antonio laughed. "I'll bet I do."

After downing his drink in one long swallow, Constanzo pointed at the door. "Let's get going. I don't want to end up in a crush of reporters like we did the last time we went somewhere."

Antonio straightened his tie one more time. "Hey, you made me the paparazzi monster I am today."

"You are not a monster." The lilt of an Italian accent warmed his father's voice. "You could be one of the most important painters of the twenty-first century. You are a talent."

He knew that, of course. But having talent wasn't what most people imagined. He didn't put his gift away in a shiny box and take it out when he needed it. Talent, the need to paint, the breathtaking yearning to explore life on a canvas, were what drove him. But for the past two years he hadn't even been able to pick up a brush. Forget about painting, accepting commissions, having a purpose in life. Now, he ate, drank, slept—but didn't really live. Because he'd made millions on his art in the past few years, and, with his savvy businessman father's help, he'd parlayed those millions into hundreds of millions through investments, money wasn't an issue. He had the freedom and the resources to ignore his calling.

The private elevator door silently opened. Antonio and his father stepped inside. Constanzo sighed. "If you had a personal assistant, this wouldn't have happened."

Antonio worked to hide a wince. He didn't have to ask what his father meant. He knew. "I'm sorry."

"I wanted you to be the artist who did the murals for Tucker's new building. Those works would have been seen by thousands of people. Ordinary people. You would have brought art to the masses in a concrete way. But you missed the deadline."

"I don't have a brain for remembering dates."

"Which is exactly why you need a personal assistant."

Antonio fought the urge to squeeze his eyes shut. What he needed was to be left alone. Or maybe to roll back the clock so far that he hadn't married the woman who'd betrayed him. But that wasn't going to happen. He was stuck in a combination of grief and guilt that paralyzed him.

Constanzo's limousine awaited them on the street. They walked under the building portico without speaking. Antonio motioned for his father to enter first.

When he slid in behind him, soft white leather greeted him. A discreet minibar sat near the media controls. His father hit a few buttons and classical music quietly entered the space.

The driver closed the door and in less than a minute the limo pulled onto the street.

"A PA could also handle some of the Gisella problems that remain."

Antonio's jaw twitched.

Constanzo sighed. "Well, you don't seem to want to handle them." He sighed again, more deeply this time. "Antonio, it's been two years. You cannot grieve forever."

Antonio glanced at his father. He let his lips lift into a small smile. Pretending he was grieving had been the only way he'd survived the years since his wife's death. Beautiful Gisella had burst into his life like a whirlwind. Twenty-four hours after they'd met they'd been in bed. Twenty-four weeks after that they were married. He'd been so smitten, so hopelessly in love, that days, weeks, months hadn't mattered. But looking back, he recognized the signs he should have seen. Her modeling career hadn't tanked, but it had been teetering, and marriage to the newly famous Italian painter had put her in the limelight again. Her sudden interest in international causes hadn't cropped up until she found a way to use them to keep herself, her name, in the papers and on everybody's lips. She'd even spoken at the UN. He'd been so proud...so stupid.

"My son, I know adult children don't like nagging, meddling parents, but this time I am correct. You must move on."

Without replying, he looked out the window at the hustle and bustle of New York City in the spring. Bumper-to-bumper traffic, most of it taxicabs. Optimistic residents walking up and down the sidewalk in lightweight coats. The sun glittering off the glass of towering buildings. At one time he'd loved this city more than he'd loved the

Italian countryside that was his home. But she'd even ruined that for him.

"Please do not spoil Ricky and Eloise's day with
your sadness."

"I'm not sad, Dad. I'm fine."

The limo stopped. They exited and headed into the
enormous gray stone cathedral.

The ceremony was long and Antonio's mind wandered to his own wedding, in this same church, to a
woman who hadn't really loved him.

No, he wasn't sad. He was angry, so furious some
days his heart beat slow and heavy with it. But he
couldn't ruin the reputation of a woman who'd used
him to become a cultural icon any more than he could
pretend she'd been the perfect wife she'd portrayed.

Which meant he couldn't have a PA digging through
papers in his office or documents on his computer.

The ceremony ended. The priest said, "I now intro-
duce Mr. and Mrs. Richard Langley."

His best friend, Ricky, and his beautiful new wife,
Eloise, turned and faced the crowd of friends and rel-
atives sitting in the pews. A round of applause burst
through the church and Ricky and Eloise headed down
the aisle. Matron of honor Olivia Engle and best man
Tucker Engle, also husband and wife, followed them
out of the church. Antonio walked to the center aisle
to meet his partner, Laura Beth Matthews.

Laura Beth was a sweet young woman he'd met and
had gotten to know fairly well over the years when she'd
visited Olivia and Tucker at their Italian villa, and every
time there was a baptism, birthday or holiday party at
the Engle penthouse on Park Avenue. Unfortunately, she
had usually been with an annoying boyfriend, some-

one who didn't fit into Tucker Engle's world or Ricky Langley's, but who desperately tried to.

Laura Beth slid her hand to Antonio's elbow and he smiled at her before they walked down the aisle and out of the church.

As Ricky and Eloise greeted the long line of guests filing through the vestibule, Antonio turned to Laura Beth. "You look lovely."

She glanced down at the pale purple dress. "Eloise designs the most beautiful gowns."

"Ah, so she did this herself."

Laura Beth nodded. When she brought her gaze back to his, though, her green eyes were dull. Not sad for the change in her life that the marriage of her last room-mate would bring, but lifeless.

He caught her forearm to bring her attention to him. "Are you okay?"

She suddenly brightened. "Sure. Yes. I'm fine. Wonderful. It was just a stressful morning."

"Tell me about it. Have you ever tried traveling with a billionaire who expects everybody and everything to be at his fingertips?"

Laura Beth laughed. "Oh, come on. I love your father! He's not a prima donna."

"You've only dealt with him when you were on vacation or at a party for one of Tucker and Olivia's kids. Just try flying across the Atlantic with him."

She laughed again and something lightened in Antonio's chest. With her dark brown hair and bright green eyes, Laura Beth was much too pretty to be so—

He paused, not able to put a label on her mood. Nervous didn't quite hit the mark. Unhappy wasn't it either. She seemed more like distant. As if she were preoccupied.

Seeing Ricky and Eloise still had a line of guests filing out of the church, he said, "So what's up?"

Her head snapped in his direction. "Up?"

"You're here one minute, but your mind is gone the next. You're obviously mulling something over. Or trying to figure something out."

"I…um…well, I have to be out of my apartment tomorrow before noon."

His eyebrows rose. "And you're not packed?"

"No, I'm packed. I just don't have anywhere to go."

"You could stay at Constanzo's penthouse. We leave tomorrow morning."

She blushed. "Yeah, I could stay at Tucker and Olivia's, too." The red of her face deepened. "I'm always taking advantage of other people's goodwill."

The greeting line for wedding guests suddenly ended. Ricky and Eloise headed outside. Antonio caught Laura Beth's hand and led her to the side door. "Let's go. We want to be outside to toss confetti when they come out."

When Antonio took her hand and guided her out into the warm spring day, Laura Beth's heart tugged. With his shoulder-length curly black hair and penetrating dark eyes, he was the epitome of the sexy artist. But that wasn't why her heart skipped a beat. His very casual way of making her feel a part of things, when her brain kept dragging her away, lifted her spirits. He was a good man, with a big heart and so much talent she almost couldn't fathom it.

She'd had a crush on him from the day she'd met him. But she'd been dating Bruce. Then Antonio had gotten married, and two short years after that he was mourning the loss of his beautiful, equally talented, dedicated wife. So though she'd crushed on him, she'd never even let the thought of flirting with him fully form. And now, pregnant, she only let the thought flit through her brain. She absolutely wouldn't act on it.

She should just get off her self-pity train and help Antonio enjoy the wedding, not expect him to help her.

So she made light, happy conversation while they posed for pictures as members of the wedding party, and hours later in the ballroom of the Waldorf, while they ate dinner. Antonio laughed in all the right places, but Laura Beth could see the glimmer of sadness in his eyes. As much as she wanted to be able to entertain him, she was failing. Her own troubles weighed her down, just as his dampened his mood. They'd both run out of jokes and neutral topics and even fun-filled facts. Worse, every time he turned his dark, brooding eyes on her, she wanted to flirt. Flirt! He had troubles. She had troubles. And she wanted to flirt? Ridiculous. So after the wedding party dance, she shuffled off to the ladies' room.

She sat on the cushioned sofa along the back wall and took several deep breaths. She might be able to hide out in her apartment one more night, but then she seriously had to decide where she'd sleep tomorrow. In Tucker and Olivia's penthouse? Or Constanzo Bartulocci's? Once again accepting charity.

How long could she live like this? She did not have a home. She did not have a full-time job. She was *pregnant* by a man who thought her a slut. She was a failure.

Tears filled her eyes.

Oh, great. Now she'd upset herself.

She sucked in a breath, brushed away her tears and rose from the comfortable sofa. She might not be able to pretend she wasn't in financial trouble, but for the next few hours she still had to feign happiness and fulfill her bridesmaid responsibilities.

In the plush hall outside the ladies' room, she straightened her shoulders and drank in another fortifying breath. She could do this.

The first person she saw as she entered the ballroom was Antonio, so she walked in the other direction. The pull of her attraction to him was so strong today she could have melted in his arms when they danced, and that was just wrong. He was grieving a wonderful woman whom he'd adored. And Laura Beth herself had problems to solve before she could even consider flirting with someone, let alone melting into his arms.

Walking past laughing entrepreneurs, happy socialites and waiters serving champagne, she had a strange epiphany, or maybe a rush of reality. She was only here because of her roommates. In the four years since she'd been invited into this rarified world by Olivia and Eloise, they had not only found their true callings, but they had fallen for the loves of their lives—while she hadn't found squat. Rubbing elbows with executives, she hadn't been able to prove herself enough to anyone to get a full-time job. And despite being in front of all these gorgeous eligible bachelors, she hadn't yet found a man who wanted her.

Maybe her problem wasn't that there was something wrong with her. Maybe she was in the wrong class of people. After all, she'd grown up blue-collar. Why did she believe that just because her friends fit into the glitzy, glamorous world of billionaires, she should fit in, too?

Maybe this whole mess—her inability to get a full-time job, her inability to keep her apartment and her pregnancy—was a wake-up call from the universe. *Hey,*

Laura Beth, you're in the wrong crowd. That's why you're failing!

It made so much sense that she stopped short, not quite at the open bar.

The answer was so obvious it stunned her. Though she would always be friends with Olivia and Eloise, she didn't belong in this part of their world. She was common. Normal. Not that there was anything wrong with that. It was more that a common person, someone who didn't fit in this world, would always come up short. But if she were to jump off her high horse and get a normal job, she would probably be very happy right now.

If only because she would get to be herself.

Antonio almost groaned when his dad sidled up to him at the bar. "So have you given any thought to my suggestion about a personal assistant?"

As much as Antonio loved his dad, he did have moments when he wished the old billionaire would just get lost.

"Dad, how about letting this go?"

"I think it's the answer to your problems."

Out of the corner of his eye, he saw his partner for the wedding, Laura Beth, walk up beside him and order a ginger ale from the bartender. He would only have to tap her arm and snag her attention to get himself out of this conversation. But how fair was that? Not only did he need to put his foot down with his dad, but Laura Beth obviously wanted to be left alone. It wouldn't be right to drag her into his drama.

He sucked in a breath and smiled at his dad. There was only one way to stop Constanzo—pretend to agree. Albeit temporarily. "You know what? I will think about the PA." It really wasn't a lie. He would *think* about hiring a PA, but that was as far as it would go. There was no way he wanted a stranger in his house. No way he wanted someone going through his things. No way he wanted a stranger to accidentally stumble upon any of his wife's deceit when rummaging through papers or files or phone records while trying to organize him.

Constanzo's face lit. "You will?"

"Sure."

"And maybe start painting again?"

He stole a glance at Laura Beth, suddenly wishing he could capture that faraway look in her eyes, the expression that was half-wistful, half-sad. She was so naturally beautiful. High cheekbones gave her face a sculpted look that would serve her well as she aged. And her bounty of hair? He could see himself undoing that fancy hairdo and fanning his fingers through the silken strands to loosen it, right before he kissed her.

What? Where had that come from?

He shook his head to clear it, deciding it was time to get away from his dad before he had any more crazy thoughts.

He faced Constanzo. "I'll paint when I paint. Now, I need to get mingling again."

As he walked away from the bar, he noticed his dad bridging the gap between himself and Laura Beth and sighed with relief. This meant his dad wouldn't follow him. Besides which, it would help Laura Beth get her mind off her troubles. When he wasn't hounding Antonio about something or another in his life, Constanzo Bartulocci could be a very funny guy.

Laura Beth glanced at Constanzo and pasted a smile on her face. Now that she recognized she didn't belong in this crowd, that she was pretending to be someone she wasn't, she knew exactly what to do: enjoy the rest of the wedding, then get busy finding a normal job and some new roommates. Whoever she chose couldn't ever replace Olivia and Eloise—no one would ever replace her two best friends—but she'd make it work.

"You seem sad tonight."

Laura Beth nodded and smiled at Constanzo. He was like everybody's rich uncle. But he didn't flaunt his money. He made people laugh. He'd made *her* laugh at more than one of Olivia and Tucker's family events. It wasn't unusual or out of line for her to confide. She simply wouldn't tell him everything.

"My second roommate got married today," she said, taking advantage of the obvious. "I'm not exactly an old maid, but I'm on the road."

Constanzo laughed. "You Americans. What is this old maid thing? Can't a woman mature and enjoy life without being married?"

She laughed lightly. That was exactly the attitude she needed to cultivate. "Actually, yes, she can."

"Good. A woman doesn't need a man. She should *want* a man in her life. But he should complement her, not define her."

She toasted him with her glass of ginger ale. "Wise words."

"So, now that we've settled the old maid issue, what else has made you sad?"

"I'm fine."

He studied her face, then shook his head. "I don't think so."

"Jeez. You're as perceptive as Antonio."

"Where do you think he gets it?"

"I thought it was the artist in him."

Constanzo shook his head sadly. "Unfortunately,

since his wife's death, I think the artist in my son is withering and dying."

His gaze drifted to Antonio, and Laura Beth followed his line of sight. Antonio was stunning in his tuxedo, with his hair a little wild. Every woman he passed eyed him with interest. The spark of her crush lit again, the desire to walk over and suggest another dance rising up in her. But that was wrong. Not only did she have troubles she had to solve before she got involved with another man, but as every woman around him drooled, Antonio didn't seem to see anybody.

"The death of a spouse is difficult."

Constanzo accepted that with a slight nod of his head. "I don't want him to lose his entire life over this."

"He'll come around."

"He needs a nudge."

Laura Beth laughed. "A nudge?"

Constanzo sucked in a breath. "Yes, he needs to hire help. An assistant. Somebody who can live with him and get him on track."

"Sounds like a tall order."

"I don't think so. We've been talking about him hiring a personal assistant, and he's finally agreeable, which means he's finally ready to heal and get back into life. I think once an assistant gets rid of the two years of junk he's let accumulate in his office, Antonio will be able to see his future—not his past."

Laura Beth mulled that over for a second. "Oddly, Constanzo, that actually makes sense."

Constanzo laughed. "I like that you understand us. It's part of why I find you to chat to at parties."

She smiled. "There's not much to understand. You're a dad who loves his son. He's a son who appreciates having a dad. All the rest is just stuff."

He laughed again. "I wish I could hire you to be his PA."

Laura Beth paused her ginger ale halfway to her lips.

"But I'm sure you wouldn't want to live in Italy. And then there's matter of the job itself. I'm sure you're accustomed to much loftier employment."

She sniffed a laugh. "My degree has gotten me nothing but temp jobs."

His eyebrows rose. "So you're interested?"

She thought that through. A real full-time job, that came with room and board? In a country away from her family and friends, so she could think through what to do about her pregnancy before she announced it?

"Yes. I'm interested."

CHAPTER TWO

THE NEXT MORNING, as instructed by Constanzo, Laura Beth took a taxi to Tucker Engle's private airstrip. She pulled her measly suitcase out of the backseat and paid the driver one-fifth of the money she had, leaving her a mere pittance. If this job didn't pan out, she'd be penniless. But since she was already in trouble, and knew Antonio and Constanzo well, taking work as Antonio's personal assistant wasn't much of a risk.

A swirl of April air kicked up dust on the tarmac as she walked to the plane. Two pilots stood beside the lowered stairway, comparing information in logbooks. As she approached, one of the men saw her and smiled. He said something in Italian and she winced.

"Sorry. I don't speak Italian."

The pilot laughed. "I speak English. What can we do for you?"

"I'm Laura Beth Matthews. Constanzo told me he would call you to add my name to your passenger list."

The pilot looked down, then back up again. But the second pilot pointed at the list.

"Ah, *sì*. Here you are." He reached for her pathetic suitcase. "I will take care of this."

Fear ruffled through her as a man she didn't know

took the entirety of her possessions out of her hand and walked away. But the second pilot pointed up the steps.

She sucked in a breath. She needed to get away. She needed time to think. She needed a job. She climbed the stairs.

At the doorway she stopped and gasped. The main area looked more like a living room than a plane. Rows of seats had been replaced by long, comfortable-looking sofas. Tables beside the sofas provided places for books, drinks or food. A desk and wet bar in the back filled the remaining space.

She eased toward the sofas, wondering where the heck Constanzo and Antonio were. Sitting on the soft leather, she leaned back, enjoying the feel of it against her nape. She'd been so nervous the night before she hadn't slept, and part of her just wanted to nod off. Before she got too comfortable, though, a commotion sounded outside. She jumped up and looked out the window.

A big white limo had pulled up. Antonio got out and held the door for his dad. She tilted her head, watching them.

Dressed in jeans and an open dress shirt over a white T-shirt, Antonio looked totally different. She usually saw him in tuxedos at gallery openings or formal events, or trousers and white shirts at parties for Olivia and Tucker's kids. Seeing him so casual sent a jolt of attraction through her. Especially with the way the breeze blew through his long curly hair, making her wonder if it was as soft as it looked.

She shook her head at her stupidity and raced back to her seat. She'd just gotten settled when Constanzo boarded the plane.

"*Carissima.* You made it."

She rose, just in case she was sitting in the wrong place. "I did."

Antonio entered behind his dad. He stopped when he saw her, his brow wrinkling. "Laura Beth?"

Though Antonio had been raised in the United States, he'd spent the past five years in Italy. Speaking Italian had changed the timbre of his voice. Her name rolled off his tongue sensually. A shiver breezed along her skin. And another thought suddenly hit her—this man was now her boss. She wouldn't just be working to organize him. They'd be living together.

Oh, wow. No wonder her thoughts ran amok. *She was going to be living with the guy she'd had a crush on for five years.*

Right. Plain Jane Laura Beth would be living with a famous artist, who still grieved his equally gorgeous, equally wonderful wife. Common sense plucked away her fear. She had nothing to worry about.

She smiled and said, "Hello."

Constanzo ambled to the back of the plane. "Can I get you a drink?"

She turned to watch Constanzo as he approached the bar. "No. Thanks."

Antonio stopped in front of her. With his windblown hair and sun-kissed skin, he looked so good, so sexy, that her mouth watered. Especially when his dark eyes met hers.

"What are you doing here?"

Reminding herself Antonio wouldn't ever be attracted to her and she had to get rid of this crush, she peeked back at Constanzo again.

He batted a hand. "I hired her. She's out of her apartment and had no permanent job. It was perfect timing."

Antonio's lips lifted into a smile that would have

stopped her heart if she hadn't known he was off-limits. "Oh. That's great."

The pilot announced they'd been cleared for takeoff. Antonio pointed at the leather sofa, indicating Laura Beth should sit, then he sat beside her. Close enough to touch. Close enough that if they hit turbulence, they'd tumble together.

She squeezed her eyes shut. *Stop!*

She had to get ahold of these wayward thoughts or she'd drive herself crazy living with him! She was not in this guy's league. She'd figured all this out yesterday. She was common, pregnant and needed a job more than a crush.

They both buckled in. The little jet taxied to the runway of the small airstrip and took off smoothly. It climbed for a few minutes and leveled off before the fasten-seat-belts light blinked off and the pilot announced they anticipated an uneventful flight, so they could move about the cabin.

To settle her nerves and maybe waylay the attraction that zapped her every time she looked down and saw Antonio's thigh mere inches away from hers, Laura Beth pulled a book from her purse.

"Ah. I loved that novel."

She glanced at the book, then at Antonio. "I never took you for a science fiction fan."

"Are you kidding? Some of the best art is in science fiction. The imaginations and imagery required are magnificent."

Laura Beth smiled, glad they had something normal to talk about, but her stomach picked that exact second to growl. Her face flushed.

Antonio laughed. "You skipped breakfast."

She hadn't been able eat breakfast. It seemed that

now that she knew she was pregnant, morning sickness had kicked in.

"Um, I wasn't hungry when I got up this morning."

Antonio unbuckled his seat belt. He reached for her hand. "Come with me."

She undid her seat belt and took the hand he'd offered. Her fingers tingled when his warm hand wrapped around them. As he pulled her up to stand, she reminded herself to stop noticing these things and followed him to the back of the plane.

The area she'd believed was a wet bar was actually a small kitchenette. She gaped at it. "You have to be kidding me."

Antonio nudged his head in the direction of his dad, who had fallen asleep on the sofa across from the one where Antonio and Laura Beth had been sitting.

"Anything my dad could possibly want is always stocked on the plane. When we arrive at our destination, any food not eaten will be donated to a charity." He laughed and opened the small fridge. "How about eggs and toast?"

Her stomach didn't lurch at the thought, so she nodded.

Antonio studied her. "Hmm. Not very enthusiastic. So let's try French toast."

"I love French toast." And she hadn't had it in forever.

He motioned for her to sit at one of the bar stools, obviously needing her out of the way in the tiny space. He hit a button and what looked to be a grill appeared.

"This is so cool."

"This is the life of a billionaire."

She glanced around. Remembering her thoughts from the night before, she didn't look at the plane as somebody who someday wanted to own one. She counted her blessings that she was here and had a job and a place to stay.

"It's kind of fun getting to see things that I wouldn't normally see."

He frowned. "I don't understand."

"Well, I'm never going to be a billionaire. So I'm never going to own a plane like this."

"Ah." He broke two eggs in a bowl, added milk, vanilla and a dash of what appeared to be cinnamon, beat the mixture, then rummaged for bread. When he found it, he dipped two slices into the egg mixture and put them on the small griddle. They sizzled.

She sniffed the vanilla. "Yum."

"You really must be hungry."

"I am."

He turned to flip the two pieces of French toast. She tilted her head, taking in the details that made him who he was. Sexy dark hair. Wide shoulders. Trim hips. But his face was the showstopper. Dark, dark eyes in olive skin. A square jaw. High cheekbones.

Something soft and warm floated through her. She was just about to curse herself for looking at him again when she realized she'd never felt like this with Bruce. She'd liked Bruce—actually, she'd believed she'd loved him. But she'd never felt this odd combination of attraction and curiosity that mixed and mingled with the warmth of their friendship and turned her feelings into something more…something special.

She cleared her throat. What was she doing? Fantasizing again? This guy was her boss! Not only that, but he was a widower. Someone who'd lost his wife and still grieved her so much he no longer painted. What would he want with her? Plain, simple Laura Beth Matthews, who—oh, by the way—was also pregnant with another man's child. Her job was to organize him back to the land of the living, not drool over him.

He made eight pieces of French toast, divided them onto two plates and handed one to her.

Her stomach rumbled again. "Thanks."

He passed the syrup across the bar. She slathered it on her French toast, but waited for him to pick up his fork before she picked up hers. If there was one thing she'd learned from her years of attending Olivia and Tucker's baby events and Ricky and Eloise's elaborate parties, it was to follow the lead of the host and hostess.

He took a bite of his French toast, then smiled at her. "So getting a job where you get to live in was a pretty nifty way to handle the apartment problem."

She reddened to the roots of her hair. "Does it seem sleazy?"

"No. It's smart. After I rotated out of the foster-care system, I'd have killed for a job that got me off the streets."

"Yeah, but then you wouldn't have scrounged your way to Italy, where your dad found you."

"Scrounged." He grinned. "I love American words."

"Hey, you're half-American!"

"Yes, I am. And proud of it. I use both worlds." He frowned. "Or did." Then he brightened. "Never mind. How's the toast?"

"I love it." She pushed her plate away having eaten only two slices. "But I'm full."

Antonio took her plate and his and set them in a metal drawer, which he closed. "Staff will get this when we land."

She laughed. "Wow."

"Hey, you better get used to living like this."

Though she didn't think Antonio was as persnick-
ety or as pampered as his dad, she decided not to argue
the point. Especially since she'd had a sleepless night,
agonizing over her problems. With her tummy full and
the lull of the plane, she just wanted to curl up on one
of the sofas.

She wandered back to her seat, buckled herself in—
in case they hit turbulence—and almost immediately
fell asleep.

She awoke to the feeling of someone shaking her.
"Laura Beth...we're here."

She snuggled into the blanket someone had thrown
over her. "We're where?"

"In Italy."

Her eyes popped open. When she found herself staring into the gorgeous face of Antonio Bartulocci, it all
tumbled back. They were on a plane to Italy. His dad
had hired her. She didn't have an apartment. She was
pregnant.

Her stomach dropped.

She was pregnant. In a foreign country. Starting a
new job. Working for Antonio, who needed her. But
she was attracted to him. She thought he was the sexi-
est, most gorgeous man alive and she would be living
with him. But he didn't feel the same way about her.

That relaxed her. It could be a good thing if he only
saw her as a friend. As long as she hid her crush, there'd
be no problem. Plus, being on call twenty-four-seven to
help him get his life back would keep her from dwell-
ing on her problems.

That was the real silver lining. Not just the money.
Not just a place to live. But someone to take care of, so
she could forget about herself.

She pushed aside the soft cover. Her days of daydreaming she belonged in this world as anything other than an employee were over. She could take this job and run with it, create a halfway decent life for herself and her baby. Everything would be fine.

"Thanks for the blanket."

Antonio smiled. "My pleasure."

She found her purse and tucked her science fiction novel inside. Two gentlemen, Antonio and Constanzo waited for her to exit first.

Constanzo paused to say something to the pilots, but quickly joined them on the tarmac below the steps.

She glanced around. The sky was blue, as perfect as any she'd seen in Kentucky. Tall green grass in the fields surrounding the airstrip swayed in a subtle breeze that cut through the heat. "Another private airstrip?"

"You don't think my dad's going to have a plane and suffer the torment of going to a real airport and waiting to take off and land, do you?"

Pushing a strand of her hair off her face, she laughed. "Right. Spoiled."

"Incredibly spoiled. You're going to need to remember that."

She frowned. It was the second time he'd said something odd about her getting accustomed to his dad. Still, he was her boss now. They might have been able to relate like friends on the plane, but here on Italian soil, his home turf, her role kicked in. She was his assistant. Basically, a secretary. But this was better than anything she'd even come close to finding in New York.

This was her life now.

Constanzo walked over. "Bags are on their way to the limo."

Laura Beth said, "Wow. Fast."

Antonio laughed. "So much for you to get used to

about my dad." He nudged his father's shoulder. "Exactly how do you intend to explain to Bernice that you hired someone to help her?"

Laura Beth's brow wrinkled.

Constanzo's face reddened.

Laura Beth gasped as she faced Antonio. "You think Constanzo hired me to work for *him*?"

This time Antonio's brow wrinkled. "You're not working for my dad?"

Constanzo's face reddened even more as both Laura Beth and Antonio turned to him.

"I did not hire her to help my PA. I hired her to be yours."

Antonio's mouth fell open at his father's audacity. Anger whispered across his skin, causing his temper to bubble. He took a minute to pull in a breath and remind himself that his father hiring a PA was nothing compared to his deceased wife's handiwork.

Still, when he spoke, his voice was harsh, angry. "Why are you meddling in my life?"

Constanzo headed for the limo again. "I'm not meddling." He strolled across the quiet tarmac. "You said last night that you were thinking about this. When Laura Beth and I struck up a conversation and I realized she'd be perfect for the job, I did what I do best... I anticipated."

He almost cursed. "You meddled!"

Laura Beth touched his arm to get his attention. Her fingertips warmed his skin, caused his breathing to stutter.

"I didn't realize he didn't have your permission."

Constanzo bristled. "I did not need my son's permission. He said last night he was agreeable. I *anticipated*."

Antonio stayed outside the limo, unable to get himself to move into the car with his dad and Laura Beth, who had hesitantly climbed inside. Confusion and resentment clamored inside him. He wasn't just angry about his dad hiring someone for him; his reactions to Laura Beth were wrong.

He'd always liked her. And, yes, he supposed there was a bit of an attraction there. But suddenly, today, maybe because they'd had such an intimate chat on the plane, he was feeling things he shouldn't feel. Good God, she was a sweet girl trying to find her way in life. And he was an angry widower. He did not want to be attracted to her, and if she were smart she wouldn't want to be attracted to him. Worse, they should not be living together.

He had to fire her.

No...*Constanzo* had to fire her.

Behind him, the chauffeur wheeled their luggage to the rear of the limo. One scruffy brown bag stood out.

It had to be Laura Beth's.

Just one bag. And it was worn. So worn he would consider it unusable. But that was her best.

He scrubbed his hand across his mouth as a picture formed in his brain. Her two roommates hadn't just found the loves of their lives, they'd made careers for themselves and she was still working temp jobs.

Damn it.

He couldn't embarrass her by refusing to let her work for him. But he didn't want to be living with an attractive woman—the first woman to stir something inside him since Gisella. Worse, he didn't want someone rifling through his things.

He'd give Laura Beth a few days to rest in his country house, then gently explain that he didn't want a PA.

Since he was essentially firing her, he'd send her back to the US with a good-sized severance check and the codes for his dad's penthouse so she'd be okay until she found a new job.

But today, once he had her settled, he intended to have this out with his dad.

CHAPTER THREE

LAURA BETH WATCHED Antonio climb into the limo. He didn't say a word the entire drive to his father's house.

Nerves skittered along her skin. He didn't want her. It seemed he didn't want a PA at all…*Constanzo* did. And the second he got out of the car, Antonio would fire her.

They reached Constanzo's beautiful country home and he unceremoniously got out. Angry, too, he didn't say a word to his son. When the limo began moving again, she couldn't take the quiet.

"I'm so sorry."

Antonio stared out the window. "Not your fault. As I told you on the plane, my dad has the mistaken belief that everything he wants should be there when he wants it. Sometimes that translates into a belief that everyone in his life should do what he wants when he wants it done."

With that the car got quiet again. Any second now she expected him to apologize and fire her. But he didn't. The twenty-minute drive was extremely quiet, but with every mile that passed without him saying, "You're fired," her spirits lifted a bit. They drove up to his gorgeous country home and he got out as if nothing were amiss.

Exiting the limo, she glanced around. Antonio's

home was nestled in a silent stretch of Italian country-side. Hills and valleys layered in rich green grass with a spattering of wildflowers surrounded the new house. A smaller, much older house sat at the end of a stone path.

As if seeing the direction of her gaze, Antonio said, "That's my studio."

She tilted her head as she studied it. In some ways the old stone house was more beautiful than the big elaborate home that had obviously been built within the past few years—probably for his wife.

Her face heated as envy tightened her chest, so she quickly reprimanded herself. This man she thought so handsome had had a wife, someone he'd adored. She'd been hired to be a glorified secretary. She was pregnant with another man's child. *And* she'd also decided the night before that she was no longer going to try to fit herself into a world too grand for her. Being jealous of Antonio's dead wife, being attracted to a famous artist slated to inherit the estate of one of the world's wealthiest men…that was foolishness that she'd nip in the bud every time it popped into her head, until it left for good.

Antonio motioned to the door and she walked before him into the grand foyer of his home. A wide circular stairway and marble floors welcomed her. To the right, a painting of what looked to be the field outside his house brightened the huge foyer with its rich greens and striking blues of both the flowers and sky.

"I've seen this before."

He laughed. "In Tucker and Olivia's Montauk mansion."

She faced him. "That's right!"

"I bought it back from them."

"I can see why. It's beautiful."

"It was the first thing I painted when I rented the run-down shack I now use as a studio."

He walked up behind her. Little pinpricks of awareness danced up her spine. "The second I set foot on Italian soil, I knew this was my home, that the time I'd spent in foster care in America was an aberration. An accident." He pointed at the painting. "This picture captures all the happiness of that discovery."

"I see it."

He sniffed a laugh. "Tucker did too. Made me pay him a pretty penny to get it back." He motioned to the stairs. "Let me show you to your room."

Taken aback by the abrupt change of mood, she almost didn't follow him. Her skin was prickly and hot from his nearness, her breathing shallow. Still, she smiled and started up the steps, reminding herself that he was off-limits and she should be paying attention to the layout of the house rather than the nearness of her boss.

At the top of the staircase, Antonio directed her down a short hall. A glance to the left and right showed her the upstairs had been designed in such a way that private hallways led to individual rooms. And each wall had a painting. Some stark and stunning. Some warm and rich with color.

They finally stopped at a closed door. Antonio opened it and directed her inside. She gasped as she entered. Thick white carpets protected golden hardwood floors. A white headboard matched the white furniture, which was all brightened by an aqua comforter and bed skirt and sheer aqua curtains that billowed in the breeze of the open window.

"It's beautiful." She'd tried not to sound so pedestrian

and poor, but the simple color scheme in the huge room with such beautiful furniture took her breath away.

"Thank you. I did this room myself."

"You did?" She turned with a happy smile on her face, but her smile died when she saw him looking around oddly. "What?"

He shook his head. "It's nothing. Foolish."

"Come on." She used the cajoling voice she'd use with her older brother when he had a secret. If they were going to be working together—and she hoped his recent change in mood was an indicator that they were— she needed to get him to trust her. "We're friends. You can tell me."

He sucked in a breath, walked a bit farther into the room. "Most men let their wives decorate, but mine was away—" He caught her gaze. "Traveling. She also showed no interest in the samples the designer sent to her, and one day I just decided to look at the whole house as a canvas and—" he shrugged "—here we are."

"Well, if the rest of the rooms are as beautiful as this one, I can't wait to see everything."

He smiled slightly. "I'll give you a tour tonight."

She said, "Great," but her heart sank. Talking about his wife had made him sad. He might give her the tour, but it would be grudgingly. The disparity of their stations in life and the reality of her situation poured through her. She might be trying to get him to trust her, but if she were simply a new assistant not a friend of friends, he wouldn't give her the tour of his house. She might not even get such a grand bedroom. He probably wouldn't have told her the tidbit about decorating it himself. And he wouldn't be sad.

Maybe it was time to put herself in her place with him—*for* him.

"You don't have to." She laughed lightly, trying to sound like an employee, not a friend. "This is your home. There might be areas you wish to keep private."

He faced her, his expression filled with sadness. "People in the public eye quickly realize there is no such thing as privacy. If you sense hesitancy about my showing you the house, it's because the house reminds me of better times."

She struggled to hold back a wince at her stupidity. Of course, memories of his dead wife affected him more than the oddness of having a friend working for him. "I'm sorry."

"I'm sorry too." He glanced around at her room again. "I'd love to have my inspiration back. I'd love to paint again." He drew in a breath, as if erasing whatever memories had come to mind and faced her. "I need to go to my father's for an hour or so. But it's already late. Especially considering we're five hours ahead of New York here. You may just want to turn in for the night."

"Are you kidding? I had a seven-hour nap! Plus, I'm still on New York time."

"Maybe you'd like to read by the pool? Or make yourself something to eat. The staff doesn't return until tomorrow, but the kitchen is all yours."

He left her then and she fell to the bed, trepidation filling her. So much for thinking he'd changed his mind about keeping her. He was going to Constanzo's to confront him about hiring her. When he came back, he'd probably tell her that her services were no longer needed.

She wanted to stay. Not just because she needed a job, loved getting room and board and wanted some time away from everyone to figure out her life, but also because Antonio was so sad. Somebody needed to help him.

Empathy for Constanzo rippled through her, total understanding of why he desperately wanted to do something to lift his son out of his sadness. Antonio was a good man. Life had treated him abysmally by taking away his beloved wife. He deserved to have someone nudge him back into the real world. And having someone to help actually gave her a way to forget about her own troubles. It could be the perfect situation for both of them.

Except Antonio didn't want her.

Her stomach rumbled and she rose. Might as well find the kitchen and make herself something to eat. Because this time tomorrow she'd probably be on a plane back to New York.

A failure again.

But on her way to the kitchen, the beauty of the house superseded her need for food as it lured her from one room to the next. She hadn't expected a stuffy, formal house. Antonio was too creative for that. But she also hadn't expected to be so charmed by paintings and sculptures that added life and energy to brightly colored sofas, or the eclectic dining room that had a long wood table and sixteen different-styled chairs around it.

Eventually she found herself at the door of a room with a desk and a tall-backed chair, which fronted a huge office with an enormous window through which she could see the pool and the field of flowers behind it.

His office?

With an office in front? For an assistant?

Had he had an assistant before? Could Constanzo be right? Was he ready for someone again?

She entered hesitantly. Stacks of papers littered the first desk, the desk she believed would belong to an assistant. But his room was empty, his desk dusty though free of clutter.

She walked in slowly, ran her fingers through the dust on his desk, curious again. From the coating of dust alone, she'd swear he hadn't been in this room since his wife died.

At the wall of glass, she stopped. The window was actually a series of doors, which she slid aside. A warm breeze fluttered in, bringing the scent of the pool not more than twenty feet away. When forced to do paperwork, Antonio could be poolside.

Sheesh. The rich really knew how to live.

With a sigh, she closed the doors. But as she walked into the outer office, she saw all those papers piled high on the assistant's desk. A film of dust dulled the white of envelopes. Dust covered the arms of the desk chair. But that was nothing compared to the sheer volume of untouched paperwork, unopened mail.

Glancing around, she combed her fingers through her hair. It was no wonder Constanzo wanted his son to hire a PA. He clearly needed some assistance.

And, technically, helping him straighten this mess was her job—

If she kept it.

She walked to the desk, lifted a piece of paper and realized it was a thank-you from a fan. Reading it, she lowered herself to the chair. Obviously, Antonio didn't know the letter's author. So a simple note to express appreciation for his kindness in writing would suffice as a reply.

She leaned back. A box of fancy letterhead caught her eye. A beautiful script *A* on Antonio linked with the

B in Bartulocci. What fan wouldn't want to get a thank-you on the actual letterhead of the artist he admired?

The desire to turn on the computer and write a quick thank-you tempted her. She faced the monitor that sat on the side arm of the desk. She could press the button that would turn it on…

No. She couldn't. It wasn't right.

Still, somebody had to help him, and she needed a way to prove herself.

She lifted her hand to the start button again, but paused halfway and bit her lip. The computer software would probably be in Italian—

Though Antonio had been raised in the US—

She shook her head. It was one thing to look at a few pieces of mail, quite another to actually write letters for him without his permission.

But how else would she prove herself?

Antonio stopped his motorcycle at the front door of his father's country house. He didn't knock. He just entered the foyer and walked back to his father's game room. Sure enough, there he was, playing pool.

"I see the nap you had on the plane gave you energy too."

He set down his cue stick. "Antonio! Why aren't you home?"

"With the PA you hired for me?" He shook his head. "Because I don't want a PA and because your meddling in my life has to stop."

"I don't meddle. I anticipate."

Antonio groaned. "You meddle, Dad. And I can't have it anymore. Not just because it infuriates me, but because this time you're hurting an innocent woman. She's going to be devastated when I send her home."

"So if you're the one sending her home, how can you say that I'm the one hurting her?"

"Because you're the one who brought her here under false pretenses!"

"I did no such thing. You need her."

Antonio groaned again. "There's no reasoning with you. You always see what you want to see."

"True. But that's also why I win so much." He walked to the wall of pool sticks, chose one and offered it to Antonio. "Here is a place you sometimes beat me."

Antonio snatched the stick away from his dad. "If you win, I keep her. If I win, she goes home after a few weeks of rest. But you pay her severance and you let her stay in your penthouse in New York."

Constanzo grinned. "You're on."

They decided on best out of three. Constanzo played pool constantly in his spare time, and was very, very good. But Antonio needed to prove a point, to get it across to his dad that he couldn't take every matter into his own hands. He didn't just want to win. He had to win. In the end, he beat his dad by one shot.

Constanzo sighed. "This is a big mistake. You need her. And she needs a break."

Antonio headed for the door. "That's why I'm going to let her stay a few weeks. It'll give her time to relax enough that she can think through her problems." He turned and faced his dad. "And *you* pay her a big enough severance that she can get a decent apartment."

Constanzo sighed. "It is wrong to send her home. But I lost the bet and I agree. If she must go, I'm the one who owes her severance."

Antonio got back on his bike feeling only slightly better. He didn't want to hurt Laura Beth, and he didn't like the fact that he'd had to gamble to get his way in a situation that his father shouldn't have interfered with. But he'd won.

Revving the bike's engine, he shot along the hills, past the green fields to his house, the wind blowing his hair and teasing his face. By the time he got home, darkness had fully descended and he noticed a light coming from his office. Confused, he parked in the garage and entered through the series of doors that took him from the garage, through the butler's pantry and kitchen to the main living area.

Because there were no lights in the pool area, he thought Laura Beth must have been more tired than she'd thought and retired to her room. Glad he didn't have to face her until the next day, he headed back to the office to turn off the light.

But when he stepped inside, he stopped dead in his tracks. There, behind the stacks of unopened mail and the wide computer monitor, was Laura Beth.

He raced to the desk. "What are you doing?"

She looked up at him. "I've been sitting here fighting the temptation to read your mail." She pointed at one open fan letter. "I know you well enough that I could answer that for you. And any letter like it."

Fear collided with anger. But the stacks appeared to be untouched. The computer hadn't been turned on. She couldn't have seen anything.

His head began to pound anyway. Still, he calmed his voice before he said, "You went into my office without permission."

"I didn't touch anything but this one letter that was already open." She met his gaze. "Plus, it's my job to get you organized."

He sucked in a breath. Memories of finding his wife's itineraries and the matching itineraries of her lovers swam through him, making him shake with anger. Not at Laura Beth, but at his wife. At her shameless audacity. And his just plain stupidity. Add to that the abortion information. The appointment on the calendar. The payment in her check registry. The way she hadn't even tried to hide the fact that she'd taken his child from him.

How the hell could he face that? How could he face another person knowing that his wife hadn't even told him of the pregnancy?

It took great effort for him to soften his voice, but he did it. "I'm not ready for this."

She pointed at the stacks of papers again. "You don't have to be ready. If most of this is fan mail, I can answer it. I can create lists of requests for charitable events. I can coordinate your schedule with Olivia," she said, referring to her friend, who was also his manager. "And I think that's Constanzo's point. A smart PA could do a lot of this work for you."

"I don't want you in here! I don't want anybody in here!"

His shout echoed off the walls of the quiet office. Laura Beth shrank back, her big green eyes round and frightened.

He ran his hand along his nape. "I'm sorry. But this will not work for me." He motioned for her to rise. "Please come out from behind the desk."

She rose and stepped away from his desk.

"You are welcome to stay for the next two weeks. Rest in the sun. Be a tourist. Hell, I can take you around to see the sights. But I do not want a PA."

To his great dismay, her lower lip trembled.

"Seriously. When you return to New York, you can stay in Constanzo's penthouse. And Constanzo is writing a check for a huge severance."

The lower lip stopped trembling as fire came into her green eyes. "What?"

"This is Constanzo's mistake. He will pay for it."

"I don't want your severance! I want a job. I'm insulted by your charity when it's pretty clear I could earn my keep, and even more clear that you need me."

To his surprise, she propelled herself toward him and stood directly in front of him. The tinge of flush in her cheeks matched the glitter of anger in her green eyes. Heat poured from her, triggering his attraction. He'd always loved the way she could stand up for herself.

"I don't want to go home! I want this job. I need this job!"

She stepped closer. The raw power in her glittering eyes hit him like a punch in the gut. He hadn't seen this kind of passion in years. Hadn't felt it himself in forever. It was everything he could do not to pull her to him and kiss her senseless to capture it.

He stepped back. "You think you want this job. You think living in Italy will be a grand adventure. But trust me. You will miss your city and your family."

She eliminated the distance between them again. The fire in his belly spiked. He caught her gaze. Was she daring him to kiss her?

She didn't back down. She stood toe to toe with him. Fire matching fire. "And you can trust me when I tell you that I will not regret being thousands of miles away from my family. I need to be here. I want this job!"

He snorted in derision. He was feeling passion. She was talking about a job. He must really be tired to be so far off base, thinking a woman was daring him to kiss her when she was simply fighting to keep her job.

He turned away, started walking to the door.

Quiet, but close, as if she'd followed him, her voice

drifted to him. "Antonio, I need to be away from my family and friends. For a while. I have more than job troubles to figure out." She said nothing until he faced her again, then she caught his gaze. "I'm pregnant."

CHAPTER FOUR

"Pregnant?"

Laura Beth watched Antonio, her heart chugging, her nerve endings glittering. Her announcement might have settled him down, but while they'd argued, she'd seen something in his eyes. She'd expected anger and had been prepared to deal with it, but the smoldering gazes? Sweet, considerate Antonio had been replaced by sexy Antonio, a man who looked as though he wanted to kiss her.

The only way she could think to deal with it was to tell him the truth, and now here they were, talking about something she wasn't even ready to announce.

She stepped back. "I'm only two months along, but pregnant all the same."

He rubbed his hands across his eyes, as if confused. Whatever had been happening with him in that argument had disappeared, and he was back to being sweet Antonio, her friend.

"I'm a man. Right now I have no idea if it's appropriate to say congratulations or offer sympathy. I mean, I know this is trouble for you, but babies are wonderful." He shook his head. "And my dad? He goes bananas over babies. Boy or girl. It doesn't matter. He's a cuddler."

A laugh bubbled up. Not just from relief. He'd made

her think about the baby as a baby. A little girl. Or a little boy. She wasn't just going to be a mother; she was getting a baby.

"Congratulations are what I want."

"So the father's on board?"

She swallowed hard, not sure what to say. But she'd be answering this question for the remaining seven months of her pregnancy, so she might as well get used to it.

"No." She cleared her throat. "Let's just say his response was less than enthusiastic."

"And there's no wedding in your future?"

"He doesn't want to see me again or see the baby at all."

Antonio pointed a finger at her. "With my dad's lawyers, we can force him to be part of the baby's life."

She shook her head. "I don't want him to. He said he would send child support, but only if no one knows it's coming from him."

"I think you just blew that by telling me."

She paced away. "If he doesn't want to be part of our baby's life, then I don't want him to be. I think an angry dad would do more harm than good. And I don't want his money."

Thankfully, Antonio refrained from pointing out the obvious: that she needed money too much to turn any down. Instead, he asked, "What do you want?"

She shrugged and spread her hands. "Time. I have to tell my conservative parents that their little girl is about to become a mom with no father for her child. Ultimately, I'll need a job that supports not just me, but me and a baby. So working for you kind of solved all my problems."

He winced. "You can stay."

Hope blossomed in her chest. Being here was the perfect opportunity for her. But she couldn't take charity. "And be your assistant?"

"You're my friend. You don't have to work for your keep."

She stormed over to him. "Yes! I do! I can't be a charity case. Don't you see?"

He sighed and shook his head. "All I see is a woman with a lot of pride."

"Oh, yeah?" She crossed her arms on her chest. "What I see is a man with a lot of pride. You're fighting with your dad about hiring one measly assistant— whom you need—and you won't budge an inch! Why won't you let me work for you?"

"We're friends. I should be able to let you stay in my home as a guest, not an employee."

"That's not why you're fighting Constanzo."

He gaped at her. "Now you're telling me how I feel?"

"Before you knew I was pregnant, you didn't want me working for you. You said you don't want a PA. But it's clear you need one. So obviously there's a reason you're fighting having someone work for you."

He sighed.

"Fine. Don't tell me. Because I don't care. What I do care about is earning my keep. And just from the glance I got at your mail, it was clear that I could at least answer your fan letters. I minored in accounting, so I could also keep track of your money. Anything else in your office, in your life, in your world, I wouldn't care about."

He sighed again. "You are a pregnant woman who needs a rest. Just take the time here with me to have some fun."

She raised her chin. "No. If you won't let me work,

I won't take your charity. Not even your offer of Constanzo's penthouse. I'm going home."

"You don't have a home to go back to."

"I'll think of something."

"If I tell Constanzo you're pregnant and refusing a few weeks of rest, he won't let you use his plane."

"Then I'll fly commercial."

He raised his hands in defeat and slapped them down again. "You can't afford that."

"I know. But I'll be fine."

"No. You won't!"

"Then let me stay here for two weeks as your assistant. If you don't like what I do or still feel you don't need someone at the end of two weeks, I'll take another two weeks to rest and then go home."

He stalled, as if unaccustomed to someone compromising. His brow furrowed. His expression and demeanor were so different than five minutes ago that confusion billowed through her. When they'd first begun arguing, before he'd known she was pregnant, his eyes had been sharp. Glowing. She could have sworn he wanted to kiss her.

Her eyes narrowed again. He might have been seductive Antonio, but he hadn't made a move to kiss her. It was as if he had been daring *her* to step closer—

Had he been daring her to step closer?

He might have been. But to what end? She'd been close enough to kiss, yet he hadn't kissed her.

She swallowed just as he said, "Really? If I let you work for me for two weeks then you'll spend another two weeks resting and not arguing about going home?"

"Yes, I'll get out of your hair if you let me work for two weeks and rest for two more. But that's if you still want me to go home." Her voice shook a bit as she considered that he might have actually been attracted to her. If she hadn't told him about being pregnant...he might have kissed her. Just the thought almost made her swoon.

Telling herself it was foolishness to deal in *what if*s, she said, "But who knows? You might—" she swallowed again "—like me."

Her heart thrummed as their gazes met. He didn't seem to get the double meaning.

He broke their connection and stepped back. "Constanzo can help you find a job in New York."

She smiled sadly. Before he'd discovered she was pregnant he might have found her attractive, but he didn't now. Though something in her heart pinched, it was okay. It had to be okay. She had bigger worries than disappointment over being wanted one minute and discarded the next. After all, why would a man who'd been married to a supermodel want a pregnant commoner?

She took a step back too. "I'd have to make a ton of money to be able to live in New York on my own, especially with the added expense of a baby. If I couldn't make it as a single woman, it's pretty far-fetched to think I could make it as a single mom. At the wedding, I thought about finding new roommates, but I now realize it might be impossible to find two women who want to share the small amount of space we could afford with an infant. I think, in the end, I'm going to have to go back to Kentucky. Live with my parents until the baby is born and then hope I can find a job."

The sadness in her voice sat on Antonio's shoulders like a cold, wet coat. Two minutes ago, she'd been so fiery he'd wanted to kiss her. But suddenly she'd become meek, docile.

Not that he wasn't glad. Now that he knew she was pregnant, everything inside him had frozen with a new kind of fear. The last thing he needed in his life was someone who would remind him of the child he had lost. He might be able to keep her in his home for the four weeks of rest she needed, four weeks before her pregnancy showed…but he couldn't handle watching another man's baby grow when he knew his own child had been cast aside.

She pointed behind her to the door. "If you don't mind, I'd like to go to the kitchen to make a sandwich."

"I'll show you—"

She waved a hand to stop him. "I'm fine. I really do need some time by myself."

She turned and walked out of the room, and he fell to the tall-backed chair behind the desk and rubbed his hands down his face. The man who loved peace and quiet now had a constantly hungry pregnant woman in his home. Pregnant. As in with child. Here was a single woman with no money who was willing to beg and sacrifice to figure out what to do with her life so she could keep her child—and his wealthy wife, who could have hired all the help in the world, had aborted his baby.

He squeezed his eyes shut. He had to get her out of his house before her pregnancy showed, before the constant reminder drove him insane with sadness and anger.

But he wouldn't do it at the expense of her feelings. She'd left his office believing she'd done something wrong, when she had done nothing wrong. His jumbled emotions had caused him to react poorly.

He should apologize tonight, before she went to bed,

so she didn't take the weight of this job loss on her shoulders like one more mistake.

He bounced out of his chair and headed for the kitchen, but when he got there it was empty. And clean. Not even a bread crumb on a countertop.

Regret tightened his stomach. He hoped to God he hadn't upset her so much she'd decided not to eat. Thinking that she might have gone outside for some fresh air before making her snack, he waited in the kitchen for twenty minutes. But she never came in.

Irritation with himself poured through him. Of course he'd upset her by telling her she couldn't stay. She was pregnant and sensitive. Right now she was probably taking responsibility for everything that happened to her.

Knowing he had to apologize and make her see it wasn't her fault that he couldn't keep her, he headed upstairs to her room. The strip of light below the white door to her bedroom indicated she was inside, and he knocked once.

"Laura Beth?"

There was no answer, but the light told him she was still awake, probably reading the science fiction novel she'd had on the plane.

He knocked again. "Laura Beth?"

This time when she didn't answer, he sighed heavily. She might want her privacy, but he didn't want a sleepless night, angry with himself for being the cause of her anxiety and going to bed hungry. And he didn't want her upset with herself.

He twisted the knob. "I'm coming in."

As soon as the door opened, he knew why she hadn't answered. Sprawled across the bed, wrapped in the bath towel she'd used after showering, lay his houseguest.

Her toes hung off the side. Her hair fell down her long, sleek back. The towel cruised across her round buttocks.

The fact that she was angry with him disappeared from his brain like a puff of smoke as interest and curiosity fluttered inside him. He told himself to get out of her room. She was sleeping. Obviously exhausted. And tiptoeing closer was not a very gentlemanly thing to do.

But right at that moment, he didn't feel like a gentleman. The artist in him awoke and cautiously eyed the smooth lines of her back, the long sweep that spoke of classic femininity, the perfect milk-white skin interrupted by dark locks of hair that shimmered when she sniffed and shifted in her sleep.

Longing to paint coiled through him. Swift and sharp, it stole his breath. His fingers twitched, yearning for the slim wooden handle of a paintbrush, and also pulling him out of his trance.

Oh, dear God.

He squeezed his eyes shut. *He'd wanted to paint her.* For real. At the wedding he'd wanted to capture the expression in her eyes, but that had been more like a wish.

What he'd just felt was a genuine yearning to see her form on a canvas, to bring her essence to life.

Excitement raced through him and he studied her back, her hair, her peaceful face against the soft white pillow. His unwanted attraction to her blossomed, but the desire to paint didn't return.

Anguish filled him, but he brushed it off. He couldn't explain the fleeting moment of wanting to paint her, but it was gone and that might be for the best. His decision to let her go was a good one. Even if his ability to paint returned, he could not paint her. It could take weeks to get the image of her he wanted and by that time she'd be showing and he'd experience all the sadness of the loss of his child a hundred times over.

He quietly tiptoed backward toward the door and left her as she lay. ·

The next morning, Laura Beth awakened to the bright Italian sun peeking in through the blinds behind the sheer aqua curtains. She stretched luxuriously on the smooth, cool sheets that felt like—terry cloth?

Her brow furrowed and she looked down with a gasp as the events of the night before tumbled back. She'd been too tired to make herself something to eat but had forced herself to shower, then she'd fallen asleep before she could even get into pajamas. Pregnancy was full of surprises.

But that was fine. Today was the second day of her life as a realist. No more dreaming or rhapsodizing for her. She had a child to consider. She might have told Antonio the night before that she envisioned herself going back to Kentucky, but that wasn't the optimal plan. Her parents would eventually come around and love the baby, no matter that it didn't have a participating father and that their daughter wasn't married. But there weren't a lot of jobs for IT—information technology—people in Starlight, Kentucky, the small town in which she'd grown up. If she was going to earn a decent living, it would be by getting a job where she could use her degree. And that was what she needed to consider while she had this one-month reprieve. She had to think about exactly what kind of job she could do and in what city she would find it.

She dressed in her best jeans—which were nonetheless worn—and a pink tank top, then ambled downstairs feeling a little better. Because she'd slept later than she

normally did, her morning sickness was barely notice-
able. Antonio might not be giving her a shot to prove
that she could be a good assistant, but she needed time
to really think through her options. And he was giving
it to her. In beautiful Italy.

Technically, she was lucky.

Very lucky.

When she opened the door to the huge stainless-steel
kitchen, the noise of shuffling pots and chatting servants greeted her. Antonio's staff hadn't been around
the day before. He'd mentioned giving them time off
while he was in New York for the two weeks for Eloise and Ricky's wedding. But today they were in the
kitchen, going about what looked to be typical duties.

"Good morning!"

The three women froze. Dressed in yellow uniforms,
with their hair tucked into neat buns at the backs of
their heads, they could have been triplets, except the
woman at the stove appeared to be in her seventies.
The woman at the table was probably in her thirties.
And the woman with the dust cloth looked to be in her
early twenties.

The oldest woman said, "Good morning," but it
sounded more like "*Goot* morning."

Laura Beth eased a little farther into the room. "I'm
a friend of Antonio's. I'm staying here for a few weeks.
Hopefully, I'm going to be helping him clean his outer
office."

The youngest woman smiled. Her big brown eyes
brightened. *"Sì."*

The oldest woman batted a hand. "Her English isn't
good. God only knows what she thought you said." She
walked from behind the huge center island that housed

the six-burner chef's stove. "Would you like some coffee?"

"She can't drink coffee." Antonio's words were followed by the sound of the swinging door behind Laura Beth closing. "She's pregnant."

The eyes of all three women grew round, then bright with happiness.

Caught like a child with her hand in the cookie jar, Laura Beth spun around. Antonio's usually wild hair had been tied back, and the curve of a tattoo rose above the crew neck of his T-shirt, teasing her, tempting her to wonder what an artist would have chosen to have drawn on his shoulder. Rumor had it that he had a huge dragon tattooed from his neck to his lower back and that it was magnificent.

Interest turned to real curiosity, the kind that sent a tingle through her and made her long to ask him to take off his shirt.

Their gazes caught and her stomach cartwheeled. The attraction she felt for him rippled through her, reminding her of the look he'd given her the night before. She told herself she wasn't allowed to be attracted to her boss—even if he was gorgeous and sexy with his dark eyes that seemed to hold secrets, and the unruly hair that framed the strong face of an aristocrat. But after their encounter in the office the night before, everything about him seemed amplified.

He'd wanted to kiss her. She was just about positive of it. So why hadn't he?

Her curiosity spiked. Something soft and warm shivered in the pit of her stomach.

Oh…that had been a bad question to ask.

The oldest housekeeper's excited voice broke the trance. "We will have a baby here!"

"No." Antonio faced his staff and said, "We will have a pregnant woman here for about four weeks."

"Ah. *Sì*."

Antonio pointed at her. "This is Rosina. She supervises Carmella and Francesca."

Laura Beth stepped forward to shake their hands. "It's nice to meet you."

They giggled.

"They aren't accustomed to guests shaking their hands."

"But I'm an employee, just as they are." She turned to Antonio. Her gaze met his simmering brown eyes and her stomach fell. Good grief, he was hot.

She took a step back, but swayed. She hoped her morning sickness was back because she'd hate to think she'd actually faint over a good-looking guy.

He caught her elbows and kept her upright. "Let's get you to the dining room and get some food in that stomach."

As he led her into the ultramodern dining room, dominated by the large rectangular table with mismatched chairs, her skin prickled from the touch of his fingers on her arm.

She reminded herself that he was only a friend helping her because she'd swayed. And she was pregnant— with another man's child. She didn't know how Italian men were about these things, but lots of American men would think long and hard before they took on the responsibility for another man's child. And Antonio was half-American.

Damn it! Why was she even thinking about this?

He pulled out her chair and helped her sit, but immediately excused himself. "I'll need five minutes. By the time I get back, the staff will have breakfast ready."

She nodded and he left. Nervous, she shifted on her chair, until the pool beyond the wall of glass caught her eye. Past the shimmering water were lush gardens, and beyond that, the blue sky. She'd been to Italy before, but this place, the place Antonio had chosen, was so perfect it seemed to have been carved out of heaven. The peace and quiet of it settled over her.

The door swung open and Antonio returned to the table. "I'm sorry about that."

As he spoke, Rosina entered behind him, carrying two plates of eggs, bacon and toast. She served their breakfasts and exited. Antonio opened his napkin and picked up his fork.

"I trust eggs and bacon are good for you this morning."

She nodded eagerly, her stomach rumbling from the scent of warm bacon. "It's great. I'm starving."

His fork halfway to his plate, he paused. "You should be. You didn't eat last night. I went into the kitchen ten minutes after you said you'd be getting a snack, but you weren't there."

"Too tired. Honestly, Antonio, everybody talks about things like morning sickness, but nobody ever mentions the exhaustion."

He fussed with the silverware beside his plate. "When I told Rosina you had fallen asleep last night without even changing into pajamas, she said women are very tired for the first three months and fall asleep often."

She heard everything he said as a jumble of words. Her brain stalled then exploded after he said he knew she'd fallen asleep without changing. For him to know that, he had to have checked up on her. Which meant he'd seen her lying naked across her bed. Her face blossomed with heat.

"What?"

She sucked in a breath. "You came looking for me last night?"

"Yes."

She groaned.

He frowned. "What?"

"You saw me naked."

He busied himself with his silverware again. "No. I saw you lying on the bed with a towel wrapped around you. You weren't naked."

"Oh, way to split hairs."

"Americans are prudish."

She squeezed her eyes shut. Was she making too much of this? "You're half-American!"

He laughed. "What are you worried about? You have a beautiful, long, sleek back. I'd love to paint you, but I'd replace the towel with a swatch of silk—" He stopped. His brow furrowed.

This time she frowned. "What?"

He picked up his napkin. "It's my turn to say nothing."

"Really? Because I wouldn't mind sitting for a portrait."

He sniffed a laugh. "Then you'd be sitting for a long time. I haven't painted for two years."

Since his wife died. She knew that. And knowing he'd grieved for two long years, a smart person wouldn't push, wouldn't question any further. She reached for her toast.

Rosina walked into the dining room. "Excuse me, Mr. B. Your package has arrived. I sent it back to the office as you requested."

He rose. "Thank you, Rosina."

Laura Beth looked from Antonio to Rosina and back again. But the oldest maid smiled and walked away. Antonio set his napkin on his plate. "That would be your computer."

"My computer?"

"Yes. I ordered you a new one, since you insist on playing secretary for two weeks. Come back to the office whenever you're ready. I'll have it set up."

An odd feeling stole through Laura Beth as he walked out of the room. Why had he gotten her a new computer when there were two perfectly good computers in his office? She remembered the software might have commands in Italian and she didn't speak Italian, and went back to eating.

She finished her breakfast, wishing she could eat more. Not because she was hungry but because she simply wanted more food. But in the end, she knew if she didn't soon get ahold of her appetite, she'd be big as a house when this baby was born.

After washing her hands and brushing her teeth in her room, she made her way to the office.

As she entered, she gasped. "Wow. Look at this." Everything on the desk had been stacked in neat piles. The old computer had been removed and sat on the floor in a corner.

He pointed at his office behind her. "Everything in that room is to be left alone." He motioned to the piles on the smaller secretarial desk. "This fan mail you can answer."

"What about the other stacks?"

"Some are requests for portraits or for me to paint specific scenes or commissioned work for someone's home or office. Those we will answer together."

She nodded. Obviously considering the conversation over, he walked to the computer sitting in the corner, picked up the monitor and took it into his office. He returned and did the same with the computer tower and the keyboard. When he was done, he pulled the office door closed and locked it.

She tried to catch his gaze, but he avoided her by keeping his attention on the keys he shoved into his pocket.

"I have some errands in town. I'll be back at noon to read any letters you've drafted."

She nodded and said, "Yes," but before the word was fully out of her mouth he was gone.

She sat at her desk, glancing at the new computer, which he'd set up while she finished breakfast. When she saw that everything was in English, she reminded herself that was why he'd bought a new computer.

But that made her frown. If the computer had instructions and menus in a language she didn't speak, why would he feel the need to hide it behind closed doors?

Why hide it at all?

CHAPTER FIVE

ANTONIO RETURNED A little after three. Angry with himself for being so obvious about hiding the computer, he'd avoided his office. But he couldn't stay away any longer.

With a resigned sigh, he walked down the long quiet hall. About two feet before he reached the door, he heard the click, clack of the computer keys. He sucked in a breath and stepped inside. Laura Beth immediately looked up.

Her green eyes sparkled. Obviously, she loved to work, and he had to admit she looked right sitting behind the long, flat computer screen, her brown hair knotted away from her face and held together by two pencils.

"Love your hair."

She laughed and stretched her arms above her head, revealing her perfect bosom to him. Her pink tank top expanded to its limits. The long lines of her slender neck all but outlined themselves for him. The slope of her breasts above the pale pink material made his fingers twitch.

The desire to paint her tightened his chest and he had to fight to stop a groan. She was the last woman in the world he needed to have in his house right now. He didn't want to give their attraction the chance to grow when he knew there was no future for them. Not only did he not want to hurt her, but he also could not handle seeing her pregnancy.

But, oh, how he wanted to paint. How he longed for brushstrokes. For the joy of finding just the right light, just the right angle…and he could see all of it with her.

She pointed at her head. "I forgot that my hair gets in my way. So I had to improvise."

She lowered her arms and his vision of painting her crumbled like the walls of the Coliseum. One second the urge to paint was so strong he could see the brushstrokes in his mind's eye; the next minute it was gone and in its wake was a cold, hollow space.

He wanted to curse. He'd finally gotten adjusted to not painting. He'd lost the hunger. He didn't awaken every morning trembling with sorrow over losing himself, his identity, his passion.

And she'd brought it all back.

He fought the impulse to turn and walk out of the office, telling himself anything to do with painting wasn't Laura Beth's fault. These were his demons, left behind by the betrayal of a narcissistic wife and his own stupidity in tumbling into a disastrous marriage with her. He couldn't take any of this out on Laura Beth.

As casually as possible, he said, "Well, your hair is certainly interesting." He motioned to the stacks of letters. "I see you made headway."

"It's fun pretending to be you, thanking people for adoring my work."

He sniffed a laugh and leaned his hip against the corner of the desk. "Give me a pen and I'll sign them."

Like a good assistant, she rummaged for a pen. When she found one, she handed it to him along with the first stack of replies to fan letters. He looked down only long enough to find the place for his signature, then began writing.

He'd signed three letters before she grabbed the stack and pulled it away from him.

A look of sheer horror darkened her face. "You're not reading them!"

"I don't need to read them. I trust you."

"That's nice, but aren't you at least a little curious about what I'm telling people?"

"No. I assume you're saying thanks, and that you homed in on some detail of their letter to me, some comment, and you addressed that to make each letter sound personal."

She fell back to her chair. "Yes. But you should still want to read them."

He took the stack of letters from her again. "One would think you'd be happier that I trust you."

She crossed her arms on her chest. "One would, except I don't think you trust me as much as you're disinterested."

"I'm not sure I see the difference."

"I did a good job!"

"Oh, you want me to read them so I can praise you?" She tossed her hands in the air. "You're impossible."

"Actually, I'm very simple to understand. None of this interests me because I was a painter. Now I'm not."

She frowned. "But you said this morning that you'd like to paint me."

He had wanted to paint her. Twice. But both times the feeling had come and gone. Now that he had a minute of distance from it, it was easy to see the urge was unreliable. Not something to take seriously. Certainly not something to change the stable course of his life. Given that he was attracted to her and she was pregnant—while he still wrestled with the loss of his own child—that was for the best.

"A momentary slip."

She frowned at him. "Really? Because it might actually be your desire to paint coming back, and like I told you, I wouldn't mind sitting for a portrait."

He chuckled at her innocence. "Trust me. You wouldn't want to sit for a portrait."

She rose and came around the desk to face him. Leaning on the corner, he didn't have to look down to catch her gaze. They were eye level.

"I have the chance to be painted by the most sought-after artist in the world. How could that not be fun?"

He licked his suddenly dry lips. She stood inches away. Close enough that he could touch her. His desire to paint her took second place to his desire to kiss her. If wanting to paint a pregnant woman was a bad idea, being attracted to that woman was a hundred times worse. Spending the amount of time together that they'd need for a portrait would be asking for trouble.

"I didn't say it wouldn't be fun. But it wouldn't be what you think."

Her eyes lit. "That's what makes it great. I have no idea about so many things in life. I might have lived in one of the most wonderful cities in the world, but I was broke and couldn't experience any of it. Now, here I am in gorgeous Italy and I feel like the whole world is opened up to me." She stepped closer, put her hands on his shoulders. "Paint me, Antonio."

Her simple words sent a raging fire through him and the desire to paint reared up. Having to turn down the chance to get his life back hurt almost as much as the betrayal that had brought him here. But though his attraction to her was very real, there was no guarantee this yearning to paint was. He could take her to his studio, risk his sanity, feed his attraction to her, and then be unable to hold a brush.

"I told you. It wouldn't be what you think."

"Then tell me." Her eyelids blinked over her incredibly big, incredibly innocent green eyes. "Please."

Attraction stole through him, reminding him that his desire to paint her and his attraction to her were somehow knitted together, something he'd never felt before, adding to the untrustworthiness of his desire to paint. He refused to embarrass himself by taking her to his studio and freezing. And maybe it was time to be honest with her so she'd know the truth and they wouldn't have this discussion again.

"Last night, seeing your back, I might have wanted to paint you, but the feelings were different than any other I'd had when I saw something—*someone*—I wanted to paint."

Her head tilted. "How?"

He'd always known, even before he'd studied painting, that the eyes were the windows to the soul. With his gaze connected to Laura Beth's, he could see the naïveté, see that she really didn't understand a lot about life. How could he explain that the reasons he wanted to paint her were all wrapped up in an appreciation of her beauty that tipped into physical desire, when he wasn't 100 percent sure he understood it himself?

When he didn't answer, she stepped back. The innocent joy on her face disappeared. "It's okay. I get it."

"I don't think you do."

"Sure, I do. It's been two years since you've painted and suddenly you're feeling the urge again. It's not me. It's your talent waking up."

He should have agreed and let it go, but her eyes were just so sad. "It is you."

"Oh, come on, Antonio. Look at me. I'm a green-eyed brunette. A common combination. I've never stood out. Not anywhere. Not because of anything."

He stifled a laugh, then realized she was serious. "You don't think you're beautiful?"

She sniffed and turned away. "Right."

Pushing off the desk, he headed toward her. He pulled the pencils from her hair, tossed them beside the computer and watched as the smooth brown locks swayed gracefully to her shoulders. He turned her to face the mirror on the wall by the door. "Still don't think you're beautiful?"

Her mouth went dry. Her gaze latched onto his, and the heat she saw in his eyes made her knees wobble. "What are you doing?"

"I want you to see what I see when I look at you." He watched his finger as it traced along her jaw, down her neck to her collarbone. A thin line of fire sparked along her skin.

"You think you're common. I see classic beauty." His dark eyes heated even more. Anticipation trickled through her, tightening her chest, stealing her breath.

"A woman on the verge of life, about to become a mother. With everything in front of her. The painting wouldn't be simple. It would be as complex as the wonder I see in your eyes every time I look at you. And it would take time. Lots of time." His gaze met hers. "Still want me to paint you?"

Good God, yes.

The words didn't come out, but she knew they were in her eyes. She couldn't tell if he wanted to paint her because he saw something in her eyes, or if he saw something in her eyes because he wanted to paint her. But did it matter? Right at that second, with her attraction to him creating an ache in her chest...did it really freaking matter?

She waited. He waited. The electricity of longing passed between them. He longed to paint. She suddenly, fervently, wished he liked her.

Finally, her voice a mere whisper, she said, "You said this doesn't happen often?"

He shook his head. "It's never happened at all."

She swallowed. "Wow."

He spun around and stepped away. "Oh, Lord! Don't be so naive! I have no idea what this feeling is, but it's powerful." He met her gaze again. "And it could let me down. We could spend hours in my studio and I could freeze. Or your portrait could be the most exciting, most important of my life."

"Antonio, if you're trying to dissuade me, you're going at it all wrong. What woman in the world wouldn't want to hear that?"

"You shouldn't!" The words were hot, clipped. "This feeling could be nothing but my talent tormenting me." He picked up the stack of letters. "Go freshen up for dinner while I sign these."

She stayed where she stood, frozen, suddenly understanding. To him she wasn't an opportunity, but a torment.

"Now!"

She pivoted and raced from the room, but even before she reached the stairs she'd decided Antonio was wrong. He couldn't know that he would freeze unless he tried to paint her.

She might have lost tonight's fight, but the next time they had this discussion, she wouldn't lose.

They managed to get through dinner by skirting the elephant in the room. He feared picking up a brush and she longed for him to paint her. Or maybe she was just curious. After all, Bruce dumping her had made her feel worthless. She'd spent every moment of every date trying to get Bruce to say something special, something romantic, and she'd failed. But Antonio wanted to paint her. He thought she was classically beautiful. That her painting might become the most important of his life.

She knew he hadn't meant it as romantic, but she was so starved for affection that it felt romantic. And she was supposed to ignore it? Not want it? Not be curious?

But that night in her bed, she scolded herself for being such a schoolgirl. Yes, she'd never had a man think her beautiful enough to be a work of art. And, yes, she'd never been attracted to anyone the way she was to Antonio…but was that good? Or bad? She was a pregnant woman with responsibilities to think about. She shouldn't be daydreaming. Fantasizing.

She spent an almost sleepless night, and in the morning groaned when she knew she had to get up. The truth was Antonio would probably like it if she slept in and didn't do any work. They both knew the job was temporary. She was going home in a few weeks. He didn't want the feelings that he had around her, and her going home would settle all that for him.

But like it or not, Antonio needed a PA and she had a baby to support. She should have been able to prove herself and keep this job, but that crazy feeling or need he had to paint her had ruined everything.

She pulled a pair of old, worn jeans and a big gray

T-shirt from her closet. The staff might wear uniforms, but Antonio wore T-shirts—

An idea came and her eyes narrowed as she thought it through. She dug through her clothes until she found her three skirts, three pairs of dress trousers and a few tops that she typically wore for work. This might be Italy, and Antonio might dress like a beach bum, but she was supposed to be a PA. Maybe if she dressed like one, he'd stop wanting to paint her and see her as the worker she was supposed to be.

She slipped into a gray skirt and white blouse that looked like a man's shirt, pulled her hair back into a bun at her nape, sans pencils this time, and slid into gray flats. Instead of her contacts, she wore brown-framed glasses.

Antonio wasn't at breakfast that morning, so she ate quickly and headed for the office. He wasn't there either. But that was fine. She still had plenty of fan letters to answer. She ate lunch alone, fighting the urge to ask Rosina if she knew where Antonio was. She was a secretary, not his girlfriend. Or even his friend. If she wanted to keep her job, then she couldn't see herself as his friend anymore. She had to work the job correctly. Not insinuate herself into his life.

Not secretly long for a relationship with him.

But when he wasn't there at supper time or for breakfast the next morning, she got nervous, antsy. What if his plan was to avoid her for two weeks, tell her the PA thing hadn't worked out and give her another two weeks of alone time to rest? What if she was working to prove herself when there really was no possibility of her keeping this job?

In the office, she lifted the final three fan letters. In an hour, she'd have nothing to do. She answered the last pieces of fan mail and set the letters on top of the stack she'd generated the day before.

He hadn't even come in to sign the letters.

Where was he?

Was she going to let him avoid her so he could take the easy way out? Just send her off with a pat on her head?

She straightened her shoulders. She'd be damned if yet another man would send her off with a pat on her head. And if she had to drag him into this office by the scruff of the neck, he would see that one of two things was going to happen here. Either he would let her work for him—really work—or she was going home. She did not take charity.

Still, she needed the job more than her pride. She was not going to let him slide out of giving her a chance to prove herself by avoiding her. He was going to answer the requests for commissioned paintings with her. He was going to do his job, damn it!

All fired up, she marched out of the office and into the kitchen. "Rosina?"

The maid looked up. *"Sì?"*

"Where is Mr. Bartulocci?"

She frowned. "He say not to tell you."

She shoved her shoulders back even farther. "Oh, really? Would you like me to tell his father that you stood in the way of him getting the help in his office that he needs?"

"No, ma'am."

"Then let me suggest you tell me where he is."

Rosina sighed. "Mr. Constanzo might be bossy, but Antonio is my boss."

She spun on her heel. "Fine. Then I'll simply find him myself."

"Okay. Just don't go into his studio."

Her hand on the swinging door, Laura Beth paused, turned and faced Rosina. "His studio?"

Rosina went back to kneading her bread. "I said nothing."

Laura Beth's lips rose slowly. "I wasn't even in the kitchen."

His strong reaction to painting her had led her to believe his studio would be the last place he'd want to be. So it confused her that he'd be in the old, crumbling house that reminded him he couldn't paint.

But whatever. The plan was to find him, no matter where he was, and force him to see she could be a good employee for him.

It took a few minutes to locate the door that led to the studio. The old stone path had been repaired, but appeared to be the original walkway. The house's door was so old the bottom looked to have been gnawed by wild animals. She tried the knob and it moved, granting her entrance.

The cluttered front room held everything *but* canvases and frames. Paint cans—not artist's paint, but house paint—sat on the floor. Strips of fabric lay haphazardly on metal shelves. She recognized one of the swatches as the fabric for one of the chairs in his dining room.

She glanced around. Most of this stuff corresponded to something in his house. He'd stored leftovers and castoffs here.

He'd said he hadn't painted since his wife's death. But if the items in this room were any indicator, it had been longer than that.

She stepped over a small stack of lumber and around some paint cans and walked through a door that took her into the huge back room, empty save for Antonio, who sat on a stool, staring at a blank canvas.

Light poured in from a bank of windows on the back wall and set the entire room aglow. She didn't know much about painting, but she imagined lots of light was essential.

"Think of the devil and look who appears."

She walked a little farther into the room. "Are you calling me Satan?"

"I'm telling you I was thinking about you."

In a room with a blank canvas.

Because he wanted to paint her.

Because he thought she was classically beautiful.

Tingles pirouetted along her skin. She told herself to ignore them. He didn't want what he felt for her and she did want this job. Acting like a PA had jarred her out of her feelings, so maybe forcing him to see her as a PA would jar him out of his.

She cleared her throat. "I have nothing to do."

He sucked in a long breath and said, "Fine," as he turned on the stool. But when he saw her, he burst out laughing. "Trying to tune in to my librarian fantasy?"

She pushed her glasses up her nose. "I'm trying to look like a PA so I get a fair shot at working for you."

He rose from the stool and walked toward her, stopping mere inches in front of her. "You still want to work for me?"

Her heart jumped. The pirouetting tingles became little brush fires. A smart girl might take Constanzo's severance and run. But though Laura Beth prided herself on being smart, she was also a woman who didn't take charity and who liked a long-term plan. This one, working for Antonio, living in Italy, was a good one.

She couldn't afford New York. She didn't want to burden her parents. Keeping this job was the right move.

Instead of stepping back, she stepped forward, into his personal space, showing him he couldn't intimidate her. "Yes. I still want to work for you."

"You're a crazy woman."

"I'm a desperate woman. Your confusion about painting me isn't going to scare me."

He out and out laughed at that. "Fine."

She motioned to the door. "So let's get back to the office and tackle those letters requesting commissions."

He almost followed her to the door, but hesitated. He'd been thinking about painting her. Imagining it. Mentally feeling the sway of his brush along the canvas. The ease of movement of his arm and hand as they applied color and life to a blank space.

But his hand had shaken when he'd reached for a brush. His heart had pounded. His fingers refused to wrap around the thin handle.

"Come on, mister. I don't have all day."

He laughed. Dear God, how he wished he could get *that* on a canvas. Sensuality, sass and sense of humor. A few years ago, capturing that wouldn't even have been a challenge. It would have been a joy. Today, he couldn't pick up a brush.

He ran his shaky hand along his forehead as sadness poured through him. This place of being trapped between desire to paint and the reality that he couldn't even pick up a brush was as hot and barren as hell.

And maybe she *was* Satan.

He glanced at her simple skirt, the shirt made for a man, the too-big glasses. Or maybe she was right. Maybe she was just a single woman looking to make a life for herself, and *he* was Satan—depriving her because he worried that he couldn't endure seeing her pregnancy, watching another man's child get the chance for life his child hadn't. Watching her joy over becoming a mom.

"I'm not ready to answer the letters about commissions yet." He wasn't sure why he'd said that, except that turning everything down really was like telling the world his career was over. "But maybe it's time I looked at some of the invitations."

"Invitations?"

"To parties and galas and gallery openings." He caught her gaze. "Maybe it's time for me to get out into the world again."

Who would have thought it would be running from a pretty girl that would force him back into the world he didn't want to face? If it weren't for his fears around her, he'd be staying right where he was—hiding.

Instead, he was about to face his greatest fear—getting back into the public eye.

CHAPTER SIX

ANTONIO MANAGED TO find a gallery opening for that weekend. He called Olivia, his manager, putting his phone on speaker, and Laura Beth heard the astonishment in her friend's voice when Antonio told her he would be leaving for Barcelona that evening and would be at the event on Saturday night.

"I hadn't planned on going myself," Olivia said, her voice the kind of astonished happy that made Laura Beth stifle a laugh, since Olivia didn't know Laura Beth was in the room, or even that she was in Italy, working for Antonio. "But I can be on Tucker's plane tomorrow morning. In fact, my parents can stay with the kids and Tucker and I will both come. We'll make a romantic weekend of it."

Laura Beth glanced at Antonio, who quickly looked away. "You know I'd love to see you, but I'll be okay on my own."

"Oh, no, you won't!" Olivia immediately corrected. "You'll probably start telling people you never want to paint again, and all those great commission offers will be off the table. I'm going."

He laughed and Laura Beth watched him, a mixture of curiosity and admiration tumbling around inside her like black and white towels in a dryer. *She* saw a dark, unhappy side of Antonio when he talked about painting. But with Olivia he could joke about it. So who was he showing the real Antonio? Her or Olivia?

He disconnected the call and rose from his desk. "I will be gone for the next few days. You have two choices. Enjoy the pool or sightsee."

Watching him walk to the door, she swallowed. Had he just used work to get out of work? Maybe to show her she wasn't needed?

When she didn't answer him, Antonio motioned toward the door. "Come on, missy. I don't have all day."

Knowing she had no right to question him, she rose from her chair. "No fair using my own lines against me."

He followed her out the door. "All's fair."

In love and war.

She knew the quote. She just didn't know if he thought wanting to paint her was love or war.

Sitting alone in the huge, echoing dining room two nights later, Laura Beth felt like an idiot. She gathered her dish and silver and carried them into the kitchen.

Rosina about had a heart attack. "You are done? You barely ate two bites!"

"I'm lonely. I thought I'd come in here for company."

"Francesca and Carmella are gone."

She walked to the table and set down her plate. "But you're still here."

Rosina winced. *"Sì."*

"Then I'll talk to you."

"You are a guest! You shouldn't be in here and we're not supposed to talk to you."

"Did Antonio tell you that?"

"No. It's good manners."

"I'm not a guest. I'm an employee, like you. I should be eating in here. I *would* be eating in here with you if it weren't for my friend Olivia, who is Antonio's manager."

Rosina eased to the table, slowly took a seat. "*Sì*, Miss Olivia."

"I'm actually an IT person." At Rosina's frown, she clarified. "Information technology." She took a bite of ravioli and groaned. "This is great."

"You should eat lots of it."

Laura Beth laughed. "And get big as a house?"

"You're pregnant. You don't need to worry about gaining a little weight."

"Thanks."

"You're welcome."

They chatted a bit about Rosina's grandchildren. But the whole time they talked, Rosina looked over her shoulder, as if she was worried Antonio would arrive and scold her for fraternizing with his guests.

Respecting Rosina's fear, Laura Beth ate breakfast by herself Friday morning, but by lunch she couldn't stand being alone another second. She wandered into the kitchen long before noon and actually made her own sandwich, which seemed to scandalize Carmella.

She tried to eat alone at dinnertime, but the quiet closed in on her, and she took her plate and silver into the kitchen again.

Rosina sighed but joined her at the table.

"I'm sorry. I just hate being alone."

Rosina shook her head. "This isn't the way it works in a house with staff."

"I know. I know. But I still say we're both employees and we should be allowed to talk."

The sound of the doorbell echoed in the huge kitchen.

Rosina's face glowed with relief as she bounced off her chair. It almost seemed as if she'd been expecting the interruption. Maybe even waiting for it.

"I will get it."

As Rosina raced away, Laura Beth frowned, unable to figure out who'd be at the door. It was a little late for a delivery, though what did she know? She was in Italy, not the US. The country might be beautiful, but it was unfamiliar. Antonio had run from her. Rosina was afraid to talk to her.

This wasn't working out any better than New York would be. Though Italy offered her a way to raise her child in the sunny countryside, rather than being stifled in the kind of run-down New York City apartment she could afford, what good would it do to be raised in a home where people ignored him or her?

The kitchen door swung open. *"Cara!"* Constanzo boomed. Dressed in a lightweight suit, he strode over to her. "What are you doing here when your boss is in Spain?"

She shrugged. "He never asked me to go with him."

"You are his assistant. He needs you." He tapped her chair twice. "Go pack."

She gaped at him. "Go pack? No way! Antonio will be really mad at me if I just pop up in Barcelona!"

"Then you will go as my guest. You can't sit around here moping for days."

She'd actually thought something similar sitting by the pool that afternoon.

"And since you're in Europe, why not enjoy the sights? If you don't want to find your boss, we'll make a weekend of it. I will show you Barcelona, then take you to the gallery opening myself."

Her heart thrummed with interest. She'd never seen

Spain. Still, she was in Italy to work, not race around Europe with her boss's dad. "I can't. I'm supposed to be working."

"And did my son leave you anything to do?"

She winced.

"I didn't think so."

The pragmatist in her just wouldn't give up. "It really sounds like fun, and part of me would love to go, but I didn't pack for vacation. I packed to work. I shipped most of my fun clothes home to my parents. I don't think I have anything to wear."

"You have...what you call it...a sundress? Something light and airy? Something pretty?"

"Won't women be wearing gowns at the gallery opening?" She frowned. "Or at least cocktail dresses?"

Constanzo waved his hands. "Who cares? You will be with me. No one will dare comment. Besides, you will look lovely no matter what you wear. If they snipe or whisper, it will be out of jealousy."

She didn't believe a word of it, but in desperate need of that kind of encouragement, she laughed. "You're good for my ego."

"And you laugh at my jokes." He turned her to the door. "We make a good pair. Go pack."

She quickly threw two sundresses, jeans and tops, undergarments and toiletries into her shabby bag. Trepidation nipped at her brain, but she stopped it. Antonio had left her alone with nothing to do and a staff that was afraid of her. At least with Constanzo, she'd be doing something.

With her suitcase packed, she took a quick shower, put on her taupe trousers and a crisp peach-colored blouse and headed downstairs.

She walked to the foyer, suitcase in hand, and was

met by Constanzo's driver, who took her bag and led her to the limo. When she slid onto the seat, Constanzo was talking on the phone. "Yes. The Barcelona penthouse, Bernice. And don't forget that other thing I told you." He disconnected the call. "Ready?"

She laughed. "Sure. Why not?"

Traveling with Constanzo, Laura Beth quickly learned that Antonio was right—his dad was a pain in the butt. His plane left on his timing. Cars had to be waiting for him, drivers ready to open the door and speed off, and his favorite bourbon had to be stocked everywhere.

They arrived in Barcelona late and went directly to the penthouse—a vision of modern art itself with its glass walls, high ceilings and shiny steel beams and trim.

She gasped as she entered. "Holy cow."

Constanzo laughed. "That's another reason I like you. You remind me not to take my good fortune for granted."

The limo driver set Laura Beth's bag on the marble floor and silently left in the private elevator.

Constanzo reached for the handle of her bag. "I will take this to your room."

"No. No! I'll do it." She picked it up. "See? It's light."

"Okay. Normally the gentleman in me wouldn't let you, but for some reason or another I'm very tired tonight." He plopped down on a white sofa. "Your room is the second door on the left. I'll check to see if the cook is here yet. We'll have a snack."

She almost told him she was more sleepy than hungry, but she finally realized he'd invited her along on this jaunt because he liked company too. So she headed for her room, intending to wash her face and comb her hair, then spend some time with him while he snacked.

Corridors with steel beams, skylights and glass walls took her to the second door on the left. She opened it and stepped inside.

She loved her room in Antonio's house, but this room was magnificent. Beiges, grays and whites flowed together to create a soothing space like a spa. She could almost hear the wind chimes and sitar music.

She put her suitcase on the bed and walked toward the bathroom, desperate to freshen up before her snack with Constanzo.

With a quick twist of the handle, she opened the door and there stood Antonio, wiping a white terry cloth towel down his chest, as if he'd just gotten out of the shower.

His eyes widened and he instantly rearranged the towel to cover as much of himself as possible.

But it was too late. She'd seen the dark swatches of hair covering his muscled chest, and—wrapped around the side of his neck—the black ink of the webbed wing of the rumored dragon tattoo.

He gaped at her. "What are you doing here!"

"Me?" Too shocked to monitor her responses, she yelled right back, "What are you doing here!"

"This is my dad's penthouse. Why would I not use it when I'm in Barcelona?"

She couldn't argue that, so she said, "Fine. Whatever." Lifting her chin, she began backing out of the marble-and-travertine bathroom, embarrassed not just by the fact that she'd walked in on him naked, but also because her mouth watered for a look at his tattoo. From his muscled arms, broad shoulders and defined pecs, she knew his back was probably every bit as spectacular. The right tattoo would make it sexy as hell. "I'm only here because your dad said this was my room."

"I always use this room when I stay here."

"Great. Peachy."

Her face hot, her mind reeling, she pivoted out of the bathroom and walked to the bed. Grabbing her suitcase, she headed for the main living area. Unfortunately, Antonio was right behind her.

Not about to be intimidated, she tossed her suitcase on a white sofa and made her way to the kitchen.

Constanzo sat on a stool at the center island, dipping bread into olive oil. "Come, *cara*. Eat."

Then Antonio walked in behind her and Constanzo's smile grew. "Antonio!"

He scowled at his dad. "What are you doing here?"

Constanzo laughed. "I live here."

"You live in a country house in Italy! This is a spare house."

He smiled. "It's still mine."

Antonio tossed up his hands in despair and walked to the center island. And there, on his back, was the glorious dragon.

Prickly heat crawled all over Laura Beth. The man was a god. Not only was the dragon perfect, crafted in reds, greens and blacks, but his shoulders were wide, and behind the ink of the dragon, well-defined muscles linked one to another. Every time he moved his arm, the dragon seemed to shift and shimmer as if alive.

Of course. What did she expect from an artist but a tattoo that was a work of art itself?

Oh, this was bad. Every time she learned something new about her boss, she liked him a little bit more. Deciding the best thing to do would be to pretend everything was fine, she strolled to the center island, sat on a stool and took a piece of the crusty bread.

Constanzo motioned for her to dip the bread in the olive oil. "So you and I, we go to see the sights tomorrow?"

She nodded as she slid the bread into her mouth. "Oh, this is wonderful."

From her peripheral vision, she watched Antonio's eyes narrow, as she and Constanzo behaved as if nothing was wrong, then he shook his head and stormed out.

When she was sure he was gone, she caught Constanzo's gaze. "I hope you have another bedroom for me."

He laughed. "There are five bedrooms. Suites, really. You don't even have to bump into him accidentally if you don't want to."

She sucked in a breath. Considering how much he didn't want to see her, she imagined Antonio would pack and move to a hotel the next morning, but she wasn't about to explain that to Constanzo. She sent him a smile. "Good."

But the next morning when she entered the dining room, Antonio and Constanzo sat at the long cherry-wood table, as if nothing had happened. Both rose. "Good morning!"

Constanzo's greeting was a little cheerier than Antonio's, but at least he wasn't scowling. What was with these two that they could argue one minute and be best friends the next?

Was that why she couldn't get along with Antonio? Because she wanted resolutions to arguments, when he seemed perfectly happy to ignore conflict?

Antonio surreptitiously watched Laura Beth walk to her seat. She looked girl-next-door pretty in a coral-colored

T-shirt and jeans that were so worn she was either really, really poor or really, really in fashion.

He watched her all but devour a plate of French toast as his father rambled off a long list of places he wanted to show her that morning, including the Museum of Modern Art and the Picasso Museum.

His pulse thrummed. He never came to Barcelona without a trip to the Picasso Museum. But should he risk spending time with her when she pushed all his attraction buttons?

Without looking up from the morning paper, his father said, "Would you care to join us, Antonio?"

He wanted to, but he also didn't. He'd come on this trip to get away from the temptation of his assistant, the longing to paint, when he knew it was off, wrong somehow. She was a nice girl and he was a bleak, angry man who was as much attracted to the idea of painting again as he was attracted to her. No matter how he sliced it, he would be using her.

And, if nothing else, he knew *that* wasn't right.

"I'm thinking about—" He paused. His brain picked now to die on him? He was the king of excuses for getting out of things. Especially with his father. But he wasn't at home, where he could cite a million nitpicky things he could do. He was in his father's home, in a city he didn't visit often.

His father peered at him over his reading glasses. "Thinking about what? Going to the museum? Or something else?"

He couldn't make an excuse Constanzo would see right through. It would only make the old man more curious, and when he was curious, he hounded Antonio until he admitted things he didn't want to admit. If he gave his father even the slightest hint he was avoiding

Laura Beth, his dad would either get angry or he'd figure out Antonio was attracted to her.

Oh, Lord! With his nosy dad, *that* would be a disaster.

It was the lesser of two evils to just give in and join Laura Beth and Constanzo. He could always go his own way in the museum.

"Actually, I'd love to go to the museum with you."

Constanzo's face split into a wide grin. Laura Beth looked confused. Well, good. She certainly confused him enough.

An hour later, he strolled into the main room of the penthouse, where Laura Beth perched on one of the parallel white sofas, awaiting his father. Though Constanzo had said they'd leave at ten, his dad didn't really keep to a schedule.

"He might be a minute."

She laughed. "Really? I'm shocked."

Antonio lowered himself to the sofa across from her. He didn't want to be attracted to her, hated the fleeting longing to paint she inspired, if only because it always flitted away, but she was a guest and it was time to mend fences. Even if she returned to New York tomorrow, he'd see her at Olivia and Tucker's parties. They needed to get back to behaving normally around each other. Small talk to show he wanted to be friends was exactly what they needed.

"That's right, you flew here with him last night. You've experienced the joy of traveling with my dad when he doesn't fall asleep."

She winced. "He wasn't too bad. He just wants what he wants when he wants it."

"Precisely."

He tried a smile and she smiled back. But it was a

slow, awkward lift of her lips. Discomfort shimmied around them. And why not? He'd told her his thoughts. His desire to paint her. The fact that he thought she was classically beautiful. Right before he'd chased her out of his office and then arranged to be away from her. She probably thought he was just shy of insane and might never be comfortable around him again.

She rose from the sofa and walked to the wall of windows. "The ocean is pretty from up here."

He swallowed. Her little coral-colored top hugged her back. Her threadbare jeans caressed her bottom. In his mind's eye he didn't merely see her sensual curves; he saw the breakdown of lines and color.

Longing to paint swooped through him. But he answered as calmly as he could. "The ocean is always pretty."

She conceded that with a shrug and didn't say anything else, just gazed out at the sea, looking like a woman lost, with no home...because that's what she was. Lost. Alone. Homeless.

And pregnant.

Emptiness billowed through him, like the wind catching a sail, when he thought of the loss of his own child. But his conscience pricked. As much as he'd like to pretend everything between him and Laura Beth was okay—the way he and his dad always handled conflict—she was his friend. No matter that he couldn't paint her because he didn't trust the artistic urges she inspired; he'd treated her abysmally the night before.

Heat washed through him as he remembered her walking in on him in the bathroom. Her eyes had grown huge with surprise, but he'd seen the interest, too. And her interest had fed his. Two steps forward and he could have taken her into his arms, kissed her senseless.

That's why he'd gotten angry. It had been a defense mechanism against the temptation to take advantage of what he saw in her eyes.

He should say, "I'm sorry," and apologize for yelling. He nearly did, but that might take them into a discussion of his attraction, which would lead to a discussion of him wanting to paint her and they'd already gone that route. It didn't solve anything. It actually made things worse between them.

So maybe the just-gloss-over-what-happened-and-pretend-everything's-okay technique he and Constanzo used was the way to go? Some arguments didn't have conclusions, and some conflicts simply weren't meant to be faced.

He rose, walked beside her, and said the most non-romantic, nonconfrontational thing he could think of. "So how are you feeling today?"

She cast a quick glance at him. "I'm pretty good. No morning sickness, but I think that's because your dad keeps feeding me."

"Have you told him you're pregnant?"

She grimaced. "Still working on figuring out how to tell people."

"Well, my dad would be thrilled." He would have been even more thrilled with Antonio's child, but Gisella had stolen that from both of them. "I told you. He loves babies."

"Which is why he spends so much time with Tucker and Olivia?"

"Yes. That's part of it. But Olivia and Tucker also go out of their way to make sure he's a part of things. They think of him as family and he loves that."

"That's nice."

"It is, and it works for me, too. Because any week they're in Italy entertaining him is a week I don't have to."

"Oh, really?"

Antonio pivoted away from the window to see his dad standing in the entry to the main room.

Red blotches had risen to his cheeks. His eyes narrowed condemningly. "You think you have to entertain me?"

Antonio grimaced. "I didn't mean that the way it sounded, Dad."

"I'm perfectly clear on what you meant." His chin lifted. "And if I'm such a burden, then perhaps I'll just go back to my room and wait for the soccer game." He turned on his heel and headed down the hall.

"Dad, really!" Antonio started after him. "Wait!"

Constanzo spun around. "No, you wait. I'm tired today. Very tired. But I was happy to spend the day with you anyway. If you don't like having me around, then I'll do what *I* want to do—rest in my room with a good soccer game." He turned and headed down the hall. "It's not a big deal."

Antonio watched his father walk away and turn to the right to go to his room. Constanzo backing out of plans made no sense. His dad never turned down an opportunity to be out and about, doing things, seeing things, especially when he had somebody like Laura Beth to play tour guide for.

Antonio shoved his hands into his jeans pockets and walked back to the main room to see Laura Beth standing by the window, waiting for him.

"He isn't going. Says he wants to rest."

"Oh." Laura Beth hesitantly walked toward him. "Is he okay?"

"Yeah, he just seemed—" *Odd. Unusual. Confusing.* "Tired."

"I get that. He didn't sleep on the flight. We got in late. Then we stayed up another hour or so eating." She winced. "The man's going to make me huge."

He laughed. "He prides himself on being a good host."

She smiled, then glanced around. "So what now?"

He sucked in a breath. "I usually go to the Picasso Museum when I'm here."

She brightened. "Then let's go. I don't have anything else to do until the gallery opening tonight."

He wasn't surprised she and his father planned on going to the opening. When Constanzo butted in, he went full tilt. Maybe that was why he wanted to rest?

Antonio glanced back down the hall that led to his dad's suite. The gallery opening started late and ended in the wee hours of the morning. Constanzo wasn't as young as he used to be, and he might have realized he couldn't waste his energy today if he intended to be up until three. Maybe he knew he couldn't spend the day sightseeing and also go to the gallery opening? And maybe the whole nonargument they'd just had was his way of getting out of sightseeing so he didn't have to admit he needed the rest.

The crazy old coot hated admitting shortcomings. Even if they were a normal part of life.

With that settled in his mind, he glanced at Laura Beth, with her bright, expectant face. He should tell her no. He'd sort of gotten them back to being friends. Spending the day with her was like tempting fate—

Or he could turn it into a day to cement their friend-ship. He could show her around, acting like a friend, and maybe his attraction would go away.

Actually, that idea was perfect.

He hoped.

CHAPTER SEVEN

PRAYING HIS PLAN to get them back behaving like friends worked, Antonio pointed to the elevator and Laura Beth followed him into the plush car, through the ornate lobby and then to the street. The doorman tossed him a set of keys. He motioned to a shiny red sports car. Low and sleek, with the black top retracted, the Jaguar hit the sweet spot of luxury and fun.

"Oh, nice!"

"It's my dad's, of course." He paused halfway to the car as guilt unexpectedly nudged him. His dad shared everything he had, gave Antonio anything he asked for, and he shouldn't have made that remark about being glad that Tucker and Olivia sometimes entertained him. But as quickly as the thoughts came, Antonio shoved them aside. His dad hadn't been insulted by his comment as much as he'd been looking for a way to bail on a day of sightseeing. Antonio was positive he had nothing to feel guilty for.

Laura Beth ambled to the Jag. Her eyes lit with joy as she took in the stunning vehicle. "Your dad has the best taste."

"Yes. He does." He opened the car door for Laura Beth and motioned for her to step inside.

She slid in, immediately glancing behind her at the

nonexistent backseat. "Maybe it's a good thing Constanzo bailed. I'm not sure how we all would have fit in this."

Walking around the hood of the car, Antonio laughed. "No worries. My dad has a limo here. There could have been space for everybody if he'd really wanted to come along."

He jumped inside. As he slipped the key into the ignition, he could feel the heat of her gaze as she studied him. This was the closest they'd been since the day he'd explained why he wanted to paint her. Hot and sharp, his attraction to her tumbled back. The temptation to touch her was so strong, he fisted his hands.

"My mom does that, you know."

Expecting something totally different from her, he frowned and peered over at her. "Does what?"

"Tells me she isn't upset when I know she is. Especially when I'm home for a holiday and I want to go somewhere without her. It's not really passive-aggressive behavior. It's more like she sees I'm an adult, and, though it's hard, she has to give me some space. So she says she's not mad and lets me go alone." She caught his gaze. "Sometimes it makes me feel guilty. But I know it's her choice. Almost like a gift."

He frowned. If Laura Beth had picked up on his exchange with Constanzo, maybe it hadn't been so innocent after all. "A gift?"

"Yes. Time alone with my friends is a gift."

He scrunched his face in confusion. "Why would Constanzo think we needed alone time when we just spent several days together?"

She shrugged. "I don't know."

"Well, whatever he's doing, it's weird, because until today Constanzo's never dropped back."

"Maybe this morning he finally got the message that you don't want him around so much?"

The guilt rolled back. It tightened his chest and clenched his stomach. He looked out over the hood of the car, then faced her. "It's not like that. The only time I freak is when he meddles."

She shook her head. "No. You're pretty much always grouchy with him. But I get it." She put her hand on his forearm, as if what she had to say was supremely important and she wanted him to listen. "You're an adult who lives twenty minutes away from a retired wealthy man who adores you and has nothing to do but dote on you."

He laughed.

"When he first found you, all this attention was probably fun. Now you want to be yourself."

"I suppose." Except without painting he had no idea who he was. And maybe that's what made him the most angry with Constanzo's meddling. He wanted to be able to say, *Let me alone so I can paint, or feed the hungry, or gamble, or read, or sit on the beach*. But he couldn't. He had no interest in anything. And having Constanzo around always reminded him of that.

Not wanting to think about *that* anymore, he hit the gas and propelled them into the street, ending the discussion.

The wind ruffled through their hair, and Laura Beth laughed with glee. "This is great!"

He hit the clutch and shifted into the next gear, working up some speed before he shifted again, and again, each time sending the little car faster as he wove in and out of lanes, dodging traffic.

She laughed merrily, shoving her hands above her head to feel the air.

Something about her laugh soothed him. She hadn't

been right about Constanzo giving him space. Never in their history together had his dad ever dropped back, unless Antonio pushed him. But suddenly it didn't matter. With the wind in his face and the sun beating down on him, it was just nice to be outside. To be away from his dad. To be away from two years' worth of requests for paintings. To be away from the studio that reminded him he couldn't create.

He sucked in the spring air, let her laugh echo around him and felt the tightness of his muscles loosen as he drove to the Picasso Museum.

Laura Beth followed Antonio to a back entrance of the pale stone museum. Glancing around, she said, "So, are you a friend of the curator or is your dad a donor?"

He said, "Both," then pulled his cell phone from his jeans pocket. "Carmen, we're here."

They waited only a few seconds before a short dark-haired woman opened the door for them. Antonio said something to her in Spanish, then she smiled and disappeared down a hallway.

The power of a billionaire would never cease to amaze Laura Beth. "Nice."

"It is nice. I don't like having to work my way through crowds or wait in lines."

"Nobody likes to work their way through a crowd or wait in a line."

"Which makes me lucky that I can come in through a back door."

She shook her head. "Right."

He led her through a maze of corridors until they entered the museum proper. Paintings dominated the space. Color and light flowed like honey. A true fan, Antonio stopped, closed his eyes and inhaled.

Laura Beth stifled a laugh. Not because it wasn't funny, but because he was home. *This* was where he loved to be.

He didn't say anything, just walked up to a painting and stood in front of it. She ambled over, sidling up to him to see the picture. Her eyes narrowed as she looked at the odd shapes, the out-of-proportion dimensions, the unexpected colors.

"Isn't that something?"

She fought not to grimace. "Yeah, it's something, all right."

It took only ten minutes and two more paintings for her to realize she didn't just dislike the first piece of art. She didn't like Picasso. Still, she smiled and nodded in all the right places, if only because she didn't want to look like a bumpkin.

Finally, she couldn't take it anymore. "I'm sorry, but these paintings are weird."

He spared her a glance and said simply, "You don't like abstracts."

She winced. "I don't."

"Why didn't you say something sooner?"

"I thought you liked this museum."

"I do." He glanced around, as if the ten minutes had filled his desire and now he was fidgety. "But today I feel odd being here—"

She didn't think that was it. As casual and calm as he tried to be about his dad backing out of their plans, she knew it had upset him. Or maybe it nagged at him. If it really was the first time Constanzo had canceled plans with him, there was a reason. And Antonio was too smart of a guy not to know that.

So why did he keep pretending he didn't care?

He looked around. "Maybe I just don't want to be inside a building?"

"Maybe." And maybe he needed a little time in the good, old-fashioned outdoors to think things through. "We've got a pretty fancy car out there. If you wanna take a ride through the city, I'm game."

Antonio cast a longing look at a painting and another thought suddenly struck her. What if his edginess wasn't about his dad but about the paintings? Picasso might be his favorite artist and he might have visited this museum every time he came to Barcelona, but she'd bet he hadn't been here since he stopped painting.

He definitely needed to get out of here.

So she gave him an easy way out. "Please. I'd love to see the city."

"Then I will take you to see the sights."

She caught his arm. "Are you missing what I said about the fancy car? I don't want to walk through museums or cathedrals. I wanna ride. Besides, I think I could get a better feel for the city if we drove."

"Barcelona is beautiful." He sucked in a breath. "Actually, a drive might be a good idea."

They climbed into the little red sports car again. Within seconds Antonio eased them into traffic. Cool air and scenery—a mix of old buildings and new, leafy green trees standing beside palms, and a sea of pedestrians—whipped by as he shifted gears to go faster and faster and swung in and out of lanes.

Air ruffled her hair. The sun warmed her. But it was the power of the Jag that put a knot in her chest. For all her intentions to stop lusting after the wonderful toys and lives of her rich friends, she loved this car.

Longing rose up in her, teasing her, tempting her. Her fingers itched to wrap around the white leather steering wheel. Her toes longed to punch the gas to the floor. For twenty minutes, she constrained it. Then suddenly she couldn't take it anymore.

She leaned toward Antonio. Shouting so he could hear her above the wind and the noise of the city, she said, "Would you mind if I drove?"

He cast her a puzzled frown, as if he wasn't sure he'd heard correctly.

She smiled hopefully. "Please? Let me drive?"

"Oh!" His voice vibrated in the wind swirling around them. "Can you drive in a city you don't know?"

She nodded eagerly. "I've driven in New York."

He frowned. "Can you drive a stick?"

"Are you kidding? I was driving my granddad's old farm pickup when I was thirteen."

He eased the car over to a space on a side street between two tall stucco buildings with black wrought-iron balconies that looked to belong to apartments. "Thirteen was a long time ago for you. Are you sure you remember how to use a clutch?"

She playfully punched his arm.

"Okay, I get it." He shoved open his car door. "Let's see what you can do."

It took a minute for them to switch seats. When she got settled, she caressed the soft leather steering wheel before she turned the key in the ignition, depressed the clutch and punched the gas.

They jolted forward and he grabbed the dash for support. "Careful, now."

She laughed, hit the clutch and shifted to a better gear. "This car is like heaven." When the engine growled for release, she hit the clutch, shifting again. "Holy bananas. It's like driving the wind."

He laughed, but he still clung to the dash. "You're going to kill someone!"

She depressed the clutch and shifted a final time, reaching the speed she wanted, barreling through yellow lights, weaving in and out of traffic.

"I never knew you were a daredevil."

His eyes weren't exactly wide with fear. But they were close. Still, she was good. She knew she was good. Driving was in her blood. "I'm not. I just like a good car."

"Really? I'd have never guessed."

"What? You think women can't appreciate a powerful engine?"

"No, you just seem a little more tame than this."

She shook her head. Yet another person who thought she was dull Laura Beth. "Right. I guess we all have our secrets." She spared him a glance. "Our passions."

He tilted his head.

She shrugged. "You like to express yourself through art. I want to be free." She took her eyes off the road to catch his gaze. "And maybe a little wild."

He laughed. "You? Wild?"

"Thank you for underestimating me."

"I don't underestimate you."

"Right. That's why you refuse to paint me. You all but said you don't think I can handle it."

"I said *I* can't handle it."

"Oh, sure you could. I can see in your eyes that you could. You just don't want it to happen."

"Sitting for a portrait can be long and boring."

She shrugged. "So?"

Antonio shook his head, but didn't reply. Laura Beth suddenly didn't care. With the wind in her hair, the sun pouring down on her and the engine in her control, for once in her life she experienced the joy of total power. She soaked it up. Swam in it. She was so sick of everybody underestimating her, thinking they knew her, when all they knew was the shadow of the person she could be with no money, no opportunities.

She suddenly wondered if that's what Antonio saw when he thought of painting her. The longing to be something more. The hidden passion.

Hope spiked through her, then quickly disappeared. He might see it, but he didn't want it.

Saddened, she slowed the car. Palm trees and four-lane streets nestled into Old World architecture gave the city a timeless air but she barely noticed it. Something inside her ached for release. She didn't want people to pity her or dismiss her. She wanted to be herself. She wanted to be the woman Antonio saw when he looked at her.

And she honest to God didn't know how to make that happen.

The more she slowed down, the more Antonio relaxed in the passenger's seat. He forgot all about her little tantrum about him underestimating her when he realized how much she truly loved driving. A passenger on Laura Beth's journey of joy, he saw everything in squares and ovals of light that highlighted aspects of her face or body. The desire to paint her didn't swell inside him. Longing didn't torment him. Instead, his painter's mind clicked in, judging light and measuring shapes, as he watched the pure, unadulterated happiness that glowed from her eyes as she drove.

But something had happened as she slowed the car. Her expression had changed. Not softened, but shifted as if she were thinking. Pondering something she couldn't quite figure out.

He tapped her arm. "Maybe it's time to head back?"

She quietly said, "Yeah."

Curiosity rose in him. She was the second person that day to do a total one-hundred-eighty-degree turn on him. Happy one minute, unhappy the next. Still, he'd made a vow to himself not to get involved with her, and he intended to keep it.

He pointed at his watch. "We have a gallery opening tonight."

She nodded, and at the first chance, she turned the car around. He thought she'd stop and they'd switch places, but she kept driving, and he leaned back. Surreptitiously watching her, he let the images of light and lines swirl around in his brain. Normal images. Calculations of dimension and perspective. They might be pointless, but at least this afternoon they weren't painful. She was a passionate, innocent woman who wanted to love life but who really hadn't had a chance. And that's what he longed to capture. The myriad emotions that always showed on her face, in her eyes.

Eventually, she pulled into a side street and turned to him. "I'm a little bit lost."

He laughed. "I think you are."

"So you don't mind taking over?"

"No."

She fondled the steering wheel, then peeked at him. "Thanks."

The sudden urge to gift her the car almost overwhelmed him. Watching her drive might have been the first time he'd seen the real Laura Beth. And he knew that was the person she wanted to be all the time. The woman who wasn't afraid. The woman who grabbed life and ran with it.

"You looked like you enjoyed it."

Her gaze darted to his. "Maybe too much."

The desire to lean forward and kiss her crept up on him so swiftly it could have surprised him, but it didn't. The woman who'd pushed that gas pedal to the floor piqued his curiosity. Not just sexually, but personally. She was as complicated as his desire to paint her.

He moved closer, watching her eyes darken as she realized he was about to kiss her. His eyelids drifted shut as his lips met hers and everything inside him froze, then sprang to glorious life. She was soft, sweet and just innocent enough to fuel the fire of his need to learn more. His hands slid up her arms to her shoulders, pulling her closer as his mouth opened over hers and she answered. His lips parted. Her tongue darted out enough for him to recognize the invitation.

Raw male need flooded him. The powerful yearning to taste and touch every inch of her rose up. But when his hormones would have pushed him, his common sense slowed him down. It was as if kissing her made him believe they could have a real relationship. No painting seduction of an innocent, but a real relationship.

The thought rocked him to his core. Dear God, this woman was pregnant. A relationship meant watching her grow with another man's child, sadly realizing he'd lost his own.

Worse, the last woman he'd been in a relationship with had made a mockery of their marriage. She'd broken his heart. Stolen his ability to paint. He'd never, ever go there again. He'd never trust. He'd certainly never give his heart. And whether she knew it or not, that was what Laura Beth needed.

Someone to trust her. Someone to love her.

He broke the kiss. But he couldn't pull away. He stared into eyes that asked a million questions he couldn't answer.

"I'm sorry."

She blinked. "Sorry you kissed me?"

He stroked her hair as the truth tumbled out. "No."

Her voice a mere whisper, she said, "Then…what are you sorry for?"

"Sorry that this can't go any further. There can't be anything between us."

"Oh. Okay."

But she didn't move away and neither did he. Confusion buffeted him. If he knew it was a bad idea to get involved with her, why couldn't he move away from her?

"We should go."

"Yeah."

Grateful that she wasn't bombarding him with questions about why there couldn't be anything between them, he opened his door and got out, and she did the same. She rounded the trunk. He walked in front of the car to get to the driver's side. He slid behind the wheel, started the car, made a series of turns and headed toward Constanzo's penthouse.

Still rattled by their kiss, he wanted to speed up and get them the hell home so he could have a few minutes alone. But he slowed the car and let her admire the architecture, the town square, the street vendors and shops.

When they returned to the penthouse, she took one last look at the Jag before shoving open her door and stepping out onto the sidewalk.

Joining her, he tossed the keys to the doorman and led her to the elevator. Neither said a word. A strange kind of sadness had enveloped him. For the first time since he'd met Gisella, he found a woman attractive, stimulating. But he was so wounded by his marriage he knew it was wrong to pursue her.

He walked through the entry to the main room of Constanzo's penthouse, and saw a huge white sheet of paper propped up on a vase on the coffee table.

He ambled over, picked up the note written in Constanzo's wide-looped script and cursed.

"What?"

"My dad has gone."

Her brow wrinkled. "Gone?"

"He took the jet and went home." Realizing this ruined Laura Beth's trip, Antonio faced her. "I'm sorry."

She bit her lower lip. "I think that little tiff with your dad this morning was bigger than you thought."

"Seriously? Do you really believe he was angry that I said I was happy to have someone else entertain him every once in a while?" He tossed his hands in disgust. "I tell him that four times a week."

She shrugged. "That might be true, but he seemed a little more sensitive than usual this morning." When Antonio groaned, she added, "Why else would he leave?"

He crumpled the paper, annoyance skittering through him. What did his dad expect him to do? Race after him? Apologize, again? He'd apologized already and Constanzo had blown him off, told him he was tired. He'd given him more reason to believe he wasn't angry than to believe he was.

"Don't worry about it." He certainly refused to. If Constanzo wanted something, expected something, then maybe he needed to be forthright and not sulk like a sour old woman. "It's not a big deal. It just means you'll have to—" *Go to the gallery opening with me.* He almost said the words, but snapped his mouth shut as the truth finally hit him.

That meddling old man!

That's why he'd left him and Laura Beth alone that morning. He wasn't mad. He must have seen something pass between them, and he'd left so they'd be forced to interact.

No. They wouldn't just be forced to interact. They'd have fun, as they'd had driving that afternoon. And they'd connected. He *kissed her.*

Oh, Constanzo was devious.

Antonio shrugged out of his jacket and tossed it on the sofa, his blood boiling. As if making him feel guilty wasn't bad enough, matchmaking was the ultimate insult.

Still, just because Constanzo had played a few tricks, that didn't mean he had to roll over and be a victim.

His voice crisp, casual, he said, "The real bottom line to this is that he took the plane. But even that's not a big deal. If he doesn't send it back for us, I have a friend I can call."

She bit her lip again, took a few steps back. "I don't want to be a burden."

He sighed. When he saw Constanzo again he intended to let him have it with both barrels, if only for scaring Laura Beth. He'd left a shy, broke, single woman in a city where she didn't even speak the language.

"You're not a burden." But he also wasn't going to let Constanzo set them up this way. As much as he would like to take her to the gallery, to have her on his arm, to laugh with her he couldn't do it. It had been wrong for him to kiss her. Equally wrong for him to be interested in her. She deserved so much more than the broken man he was. He wouldn't be a bad host, but Constanzo's plan ground to a halt right here. They'd eat something, then he would retire to his room until it was time to dress for dinner and the gallery opening—for which he had plans with Olivia. Because this was business, he didn't even have to make an excuse for not inviting Laura Beth along. His plans were already set.

He glanced around. "So, lunch?"

"We're past lunch and jogging toward dinner."

"Oh, you want to wait for dinner?"

"Are you kidding? I'm pregnant and I haven't eaten since breakfast. I'm starving. I need something now."

"That's fine. We'll have Cook make whatever you want."

Antonio led her to the kitchen, but as soon as he opened the door, he knew Cook was also gone. The place wasn't just empty. It appeared to have been buttoned down, as if Cook had stowed everything away until Constanzo's next visit.

The prickle of anger with his dad heated his blood again. Now the old coot wanted him to take Laura Beth to dinner? Well, he had another thought coming, because Antonio had plans.

Strolling toward the pantry, Laura Beth said, "I can make something for us to eat. It'll be fun."

He winced. "I can't eat now. I have dinner plans with Olivia."

She stopped and faced him. "Oh."

"I'm sorry. We haven't had a real meeting in weeks, and she likes to give me pep talks…check in with me." He shrugged. "It's a working dinner."

She waved her hand in dismissal. "No. No. I get it. This is a business trip for you."

Feeling like a first-class heel, and not able to completely ditch her, even though he knew getting involved with her would only hurt hert, he halfheartedly said, "You can come—"

But Laura Beth knew she couldn't. It would be one thing to go to dinner and the gallery with Constanzo. People would look at her and assume she was his assistant. It wouldn't matter what she wore, how much she ate, if she laughed at all the wrong places. But with Antonio and Olivia and Tucker? They would look like a foursome. Olivia would be dressed to kill, and Laura Beth would be in an old sundress, looking foolish.

"No. Thanks." She caught his gaze. "I'm tired. It's better for me to stay in. I'll fix myself a little something to eat and probably go to bed."

"You're sure?"

The relief in his eyes rattled through her, confirming her worst suspicions, filling her with disappointment. He didn't want her to tag along. They'd been fine in the car, chatty even. She'd admitted things she normally didn't admit and he'd listened. But just as he didn't want to give in to the urge to paint her, he didn't want to like her, to get to know her. He'd made that clear after their kiss when he said there could be nothing between them.

And now here she was, like Cinderella, being told she couldn't go to the ball. Even though she knew damned well she didn't belong there, it still hurt.

So she smiled. "Sure. I'm fine."

He took a few steps backward. "If you're sure."

"Antonio, stop being so polite and go."

"Okay." He turned around and walked out of the kitchen.

She leaned against the center island, disappointment flooding her. She didn't know why she was upset. So what if he'd kissed her? The moment had been right. For all she knew she could have looked like a woman issuing an invitation. He'd taken it...but regretted it. And she was wise enough not to want a man who didn't want her. She'd already had a guy like that and she was smarter than to want to get involved with another. Her current overload of emotions had to be hormonal, brought on by her pregnancy.

So why did being left behind feel like such a huge insult?

Because, deep down, she knew he liked her. Damn it.

That's what had been simmering between them all along. Not her desperate need for a job or his unexpected desire to paint her. But attraction. Maybe even genuine affection.

She pulled away from the center island and straightened her shoulders. She had to stop thinking about this. She was hungry. She needed to rest. She also needed Antonio's plane or his friend's plane, or his help, at least, to get back to Italy. She couldn't get upset because he refused to admit he liked her.

She made herself some eggs and toast and ate them on the balcony, listening to the soothing sounds of the ocean. Finished eating, she set her plate on the table beside her outdoor chair and let herself drift off to sleep.

The sound of Antonio calling for her woke her. "Laura Beth?"

She snapped up on her seat. Her heart leaped, and for a second she let herself consider that he might have changed his mind about her coming along. Lord knew she could eat a second dinner. And though she hadn't liked Picasso, a gallery opening didn't usually showcase only one artist. She'd probably see lots of paintings she'd like.

Filled with hope, she pushed off the patio chair and slid the glass door aside to enter the main living area, and there stood Antonio, so gorgeous in a black tux that her breathing actually stuttered.

"Look at you!"

His hair tied back off his face highlighted the sharp angles and planes of his chin and cheeks and made his large brown eyes appear even larger. His crisp white shirt and sleek tux weren't just sexy. They made the statement of just how refined, how wealthy, he was. Even his shiny shoes spoke of pure elegance.

"It's the first time I'll be in a gallery in over two years. I figured I couldn't look like a slouch."

"Oh, trust me. You do not look like a slouch."

He laughed, but extended his right arm toward her. "I can't get this cuff link to close."

She walked over. "Let me see."

The cuff link in question was black onyx with a diamond stud.

"I can get it."

She smiled up at him and he gazed down at her, his beautiful dark eyes shiny with anticipation. Her heart tugged. He really wanted to be back in his world. Back with his peers. His people.

And here she stood in threadbare jeans, an old top and flip-flops. Her longing for him to ask her to come to dinner and the opening with him morphed into shame. Humiliation. Even if he begged, she had nothing to wear.

But he wasn't begging.

His phone rang and she quickly fastened his cuff link so he could grab it from the coffee table. "Olivia, what's up?"

She heard the sounds of her friend's voice, though she couldn't make out the words. But Antonio laughed.

"That's perfect. I love that restaurant." He headed for the elevator. "I've got my dad's limo. I can be at your hotel in twenty minutes." He pressed the button and the door magically opened. Listening to Olivia, he turned and waved goodbye to Laura Beth as the door closed behind him.

And she stood in the glamorous main room, alone, listening to the sounds of silence.

Tears threatened but she stopped them. She wasn't upset. She was angry. It didn't matter that she didn't have a dress to wear or shoes. Antonio hadn't been glad to ditch her because she was penniless. He'd been glad to leave her behind because they'd connected that afternoon. They'd talked about Constanzo. He'd let her drive. He'd kissed her, for heaven's sake. Then they came upstairs to the penthouse and he'd gotten—distant?

She glanced around.

Why would he suddenly become cold? The only thing that had happened was finding Constanzo's note—

No. He'd become cold when they'd discovered they were alone.

And he didn't want to be alone with her.

Part of her understood. She was a pregnant woman. What rich, eligible bachelor would want to be alone with a pregnant woman?

But he had no reason to fear her. She'd never made a pass at him. If anything, he'd made a pass at her. He'd kissed her—

She tossed her hands in the air in frustration. Why was she thinking about this!

To get her mind off it all, she took a shower and washed her hair. With nothing better to do, she heated the curling iron she found in a drawer and made huge, bouncy curls out of her long locks. Before she could comb them out and style her hair, her stomach growled.

With fat, uncombed curls and dressed in pajama pants and a huge T-shirt, she walked to the kitchen. Just as she opened the refrigerator, the building doorman rang up. Though she answered the phone, she winced when a bounty of Spanish bombarded her. With a grimace, not even sure she'd be understood, she said, "I don't speak Spanish."

He said something else, then disconnected the call.

Shaking her head, she headed back to the refrigerator to find a snack, but she heard the elevator doors open, and she walked to the main room.

There in the elevator was the doorman, package in hand, grinning at her.

She walked over. "Oh, a package. That's what you were saying. We had a package."

He nodded, handed it to her and left as quickly as he'd arrived, apparently deciding she was a poor candidate for a tip, and he was right, because she didn't have any of the local currency.

She started for the coffee table to leave the big box somewhere Antonio would see it, assuming it was something for him, only to see her name on the label.

She frowned. Who would send her something here? Who even knew she was here?

Slowly walking back to her room, she examined the label one more time to make sure it really was for her.

She closed her bedroom door behind her and opened the box to find a simple black dress and black spike heels.

Confused, she pulled the dress out of the box. The material was sinfully soft, rich in texture, like a chiffon or organza. A card sat in the crinkled tissue paper that had caressed the dress. She grabbed it, opened it and read, *"Cara, go to the opening. Constanzo."*

She stared at the card, then burst out laughing. This was just too weird. How did he know she wasn't going to the opening? Unless he'd realized that she'd refused to go to the opening with Antonio because she had nothing to wear? She had mentioned that to him—

What difference did it make? Antonio was gone. She didn't have money for a taxi. Antonio had taken the limo. And she couldn't get the doorman to bring the Jag around because she didn't speak Spanish. Constanzo might want her to go, but the dress had arrived an hour too late. Which was too bad. She'd really like to go to that opening and show vain, conceited, jumping-to-conclusions Antonio he had nothing to worry about from her.

She tapped the note against her palm, then glanced at it again and smiled. It was printed on Constanzo's stationery and had his cell number on it.

She glanced at the dress, glanced at the card, glanced at herself in the mirror with her hair curled but not combed. She might look like a street person right now, but Antonio had been the one to say he wanted to paint her. Considered her classically beautiful. Kissed her. She hadn't been the one to make passes at him. So why was he acting as if she were someone to be afraid of?

Anger bubbled in her stomach. How dare he behave as if *she* was the one with the crush on him and insultingly leave her behind when he was the one who'd kissed her?

The shy Kentucky girl in her filled with fire. She raced to the kitchen and picked up the phone the staff probably used to order groceries.

It took three rings before Constanzo answered. "Hello?"

"I need a coach."

"Excuse me."

"You sent me a Cinderella dress but it came too late for me to go to the opening. Antonio's long gone with the limo. I can't go with him to the gallery."

"I will call the driver and have him come back for you."

"I want the Jag."

Constanzo laughed. "Excuse me."

"I want the Jag. If I'm going to go to the trouble of getting all dolled up...I'm making an entrance."

Constanzo laughed with glee. "That's my girl. I'll call the doorman and tell him to have the keys waiting for you when you get downstairs."

"You better also get my name on the guest list for the opening. I'm pretty sure a fancy gathering like this one is by invitation only."

"I'll have Bernice call."

"Thanks."

"You're welcome. Go knock his socks off."

CHAPTER EIGHT

STANDING IN THE main room of the gallery, pressed in by art aficionados, Antonio glanced at his watch. His return to the world of art had been a subtle, almost disappointing, one. Olivia had other clients—working clients—she was schmoozing right now. Tucker had found two business acquaintances he was talking up. And Antonio stood by a gallery owner from Madrid who desperately wanted him to do a showing.

Half of him had gone breathless at the prospect. The other half wanted to run in terror.

The screech of a car grinding to a stop stabbed into the noise of the gallery. He looked up, past Juanita Santos to the wall of windows behind her. A red Jag had pulled up to the curb for valet parking. His eyes narrowed. That looked just like Constanzo's car.

The driver's door opened. A spike heel emerged, connected to one long, slim leg.

His eyebrows rose. The crowd outside the gallery turned to the newcomer. Men smiled. Women gave her the once-over.

Antonio's mouth fell open as Laura Beth tossed the keys to the valet.

With her hair pulled up, piled high on her head, and looking luscious in the slim black dress, she walked the cobblestone path like a model working the catwalk. The dress rode her curves, accenting her womanly figure, but the black color gave her a sleek, sophisticated air. In her worn jeans and goofy librarian work clothes, she was an all-American girl. In this dress, she was a woman.

And all eyes were on her.

His heart caught and his breathing faltered, but he ignored them. He wasn't in a position to get involved with her. Though looking at her in that dress, he was again tempted. Still, for all he knew, Constanzo had set this up. But even if he hadn't, his reasons for staying away from Laura Beth were sound. Responsible. He feared watching her belly swell with child, but his first marriage had also made him jaded, angry. She was absolutely too nice for him. And right now she was about to be rejected at the door.

A gentleman, he couldn't let that happen. He turned to Juanita. "If you'll excuse me."

"Of course."

He headed for the door, his heart thundering in his chest with fear that she'd be embarrassingly refused entrance. Instead, the young man smiled and motioned for her to enter.

She dipped her head in thanks and glided into the crowd.

He stopped and waited for her to see him. When she did, she approached him.

"Well, look at you."

She smiled slowly. "You've got to stop stealing my good lines."

He laughed. "I'm glad you're here, but I'm afraid I'm—"

He was about to say *busy*, when Olivia raced over. "Laura Beth?"

She raised her hands. "In the flesh."

Olivia squealed with joy. "What are you doing here?"

"I'm spending a few weeks with Antonio, helping him try to clear out his office."

One of Olivia's eyebrows rose as she looked at Antonio, who clearly hadn't mentioned that her best friend was living with him.

Laura Beth laughed. "Don't worry. Constanzo hired me. Antonio didn't. So he's not really cooperating."

Olivia tilted her head at him. "Pity."

Then Laura Beth totally surprised him by squeezing Olivia's hand and saying, "I'd love to chat. But Antonio was just telling me that he's busy. I'm assuming you've got people for him to meet, so I'm going to walk around the gallery and, you know, browse."

Olivia gave her a quick hug. "Have fun. I do have a few people I'd like Antonio to meet. But maybe we can catch up tomorrow."

Laura Beth smiled mysteriously. "Maybe."

Then she turned and walked away.

Antonio watched the slight sway of her hips, the long curve of her spine, as she moved away from him.

"Wow. She looked happy, huh?"

Antonio faced Olivia. "Happy?"

"Yeah. Lately she's been a little glum." She slid her hand into his elbow and turned him toward the crowd again. "I guessed she was a bit upset about being room-mateless, but she wouldn't talk about it. She won't take a thing from me or Tucker. Not even a job offer. She wants to make her own way in the world." She paused and frowned. "How'd Constanzo talk her into working for you?"

He blinked. Obviously, she didn't know Laura Beth was pregnant. So he shrugged. "I think losing her apartment really brought home the fact that she couldn't be choosy about who offered her a job."

"Yeah, well, if you really don't want her, Tucker does. He has an opening for an IT person who would work directly with him, somebody he can trust with his secrets."

"Sounds perfect for her."

"It is perfect for her. He was going to make the offer after the wedding, but she disappeared. Now at least we know where she went."

"Yes, you do." And Tucker wanting to hire Laura Beth was like a blessing from heaven. A relief.

Really.

There was no reason for the odd feeling in his stomach, the fear of losing her, the reminder of how empty his house was without her.

He peered around into the crowd but couldn't see Laura Beth. Then he caught a fleeting glimpse of her as she moved between two conversation circles. The men in each cluster smiled at her and she innocently smiled back.

Jealousy catapulted through him.

"Ready to mingle?"

Thanking God for a reason to take his eyes and his attention off Laura Beth, he smiled at Olivia. "Desperately."

He spent an hour with Olivia introducing him to gallery owners, art dealers and collectors. His former charm came back to him as if he hadn't lost it. If he'd had anything new to display or sell, he would have made a killing.

But he didn't have anything new to display or sell,

and he wasn't yet entertaining commissions, so everyone drifted away. The futility of his situation roared through him, frustrating him, making him wonder why the hell he was even here.

He faced Olivia. "I'm going to get a drink. Would you like one?"

"I think I better find Tucker."

Perfect. He could go to the bar, drink himself stupid with scotch and be driven back to the penthouse, where he could pass out and forget he was a has-been.

Shifting to the side, he slid through the throng of happy people and to the discreet glass-and-marble bar set up in a corner.

"Scotch." The bartender turned to go and he caught his arm. "Three of them."

The young man nodded, apparently thinking he was getting drinks for friends, and that was just fine with Antonio. He angled himself against the marble, but when he did he saw Laura Beth, standing alone, staring at a painting.

He studied the tilt of her head, the way it clearly displayed her interest in the picture, saw the light and shadows he'd use if he painted her, so everyone would see what he saw. A newcomer falling in love.

Damn it! What was he doing imagining painting her again!

"Here you are, sir."

The bartender set three crystal glasses of scotch on the bar. Antonio took the first one and downed it. He set the empty glass on the bar, then dug through his pockets for a good tip.

He walked away with a scotch in each hand, deliberately heading away from Laura Beth, but apparently she'd moved too, because there she stood, in front of another display. This one she seemed to like about as much as she liked the Picassos.

Watching her, he sipped the second scotch. The desire to capture her slithered through him again, just as Jason Ashbury stopped in front of him.

"I wanted to give you a card."

Antonio set his second scotch on an available tray with a wince. "Sorry."

Jason laughed. "Never apologize for enjoying a good scotch." He handed the card to Antonio. "I know you're accustomed to bigger galleries, but we'd love to have you in Arizona."

And he'd love to be in a gallery in Arizona. He'd love to have a showing anywhere. If he could just freaking paint again.

His gaze strolled to Laura Beth.

Jason shook his hand. "Come visit us. Maybe we'll inspire you."

He walked away and Antonio's eyes sought Laura Beth again. She all but shimmered in the sophisticated dress, but she couldn't hide that innocence. And maybe that's what drew him. She was his deceased wife's polar opposite. And if her innocence was the medicine he needed to paint again, maybe he shouldn't fight it.

He strolled over. "Are you okay?"

"What? You think a woman can't be on her own in a gallery?"

"No. You're pregnant and it's been a long night and you still have a bit of a drive home."

She winced. "Saw me in the car, did you?"

He took a step closer. "Saw you getting out of the car."

This time she laughed. "That was fun."

"You looked like you were enjoying it."

"Oh, I was." She took a long drink of air. "I'm going to miss this."

"Barcelona?"

"No. The dressing up tonight and playacting."

He raised one eyebrow in question. "Why? You've got a few more weeks in Italy. You can do all the dressing up and playacting you want."

She shook her head. "No. I can't. Walking around here tonight, I remembered something I'd thought at the wedding. I took what I believed was a real job because I'm not an executive or a trust-fund baby or even employable in New York City." She faced him. "But you don't want me and I don't really belong here. It's time for me to go home."

Panic swirled through him. "Home New York or home Kentucky?"

"Kentucky." She raised her gaze to meet his. "I know there's not much work for an IT person there, but I'm going to have a baby. I need my mom for moral support." She sucked in a breath. "But looking at one of the pictures, I also realized I had a pretty good childhood."

He frowned. "Which picture?"

She ambled to a picture a few feet away. "This one."

It was a painting of three dogs running through the dead brush around a pond in late fall. The colors were cool, dismal. The sky so dark it was almost charcoal gray.

"*This* reminds you of home?"

Gazing at the painting, she said, "Yes."

Hoping for the best, he said, "You had a dog?"

She laughed. "No. We had ugly Novembers. The cold sets in and lingers. But some of my best life things happened in fall."

She faced him with a light in her eyes that flicked

the switch of his longing to paint. But in a different way than the day he'd found her lying on her bed wrapped in a towel, a different way even than the technical visions of dimension and light that had overtaken him various times that day. This was a serious, quiet need, something that didn't hurt him or fill him with angry longing. This one was normal.

Breathlessly afraid to lose this feeling, he quietly said, "What sort of things?"

"Well, my birthday's in the fall, so there's the whole being born thing."

He laughed.

"And every fall we returned to school." She smiled at him but her eyes were distant, as if she were thinking back to the past. "Going to school meant seeing my friends, getting new clothes, football games, school play tryouts."

"Sounds like fun."

"It was."

"And that's why you're going home?"

She moved her eyes up to meet his gaze. "I just keep thinking I'd like to be around my mom when I actually have the baby. But I also had a great childhood. I want my baby to have that, too."

He whispered, "It makes sense," not sure why the moment felt so solemn, except it meant that their time together was ending. Or maybe because he knew he needed to at least try to paint her and if he didn't ask in the next few seconds he wouldn't get the chance.

"I still think about painting you."

"I know." She stepped away. "You told me it annoys you to think about painting me."

He laughed. "Tonight's feelings are different."

She faced him. "Really?"

"Yeah. Tonight it all feels real, doable."

"Well, that's...something."

He breached the space between them. "Actually, it is. The uncontrollable urge might have been a first step, but just as your feelings about becoming a mom are shifting, growing, so are my feelings about painting you."

Her breath caught. "You're serious?"

He glanced around. "Yes. But this feeling is so new and it's only cropped up around you." He caught her gaze. "Can you spend the next few weeks with me? Let me see if I can paint again?"

"Only if you also let me work as your assistant."

Her persistence made him laugh and long to kiss her. In that very second, the need was so strong he doubted his ability to resist it. Her face tipped up to him. Her earnest eyes held his. It would be so easy.

But he'd kissed her once and it had only reminded him that he couldn't have her.

Because he couldn't.

"I want the painting to be our focus."

"Can I earn my keep by answering the rest of your mail?"

He laughed. "No. I want to do this right."

She cocked her head. Understanding flitted across her face. "Okay."

And something wonderful sprinted through his blood. Acceptance. She had needs of her own. Troubles of her own. But instead of bargaining with him, she would simply help him.

"You know, Tucker wants to hire you when you get home."

Her eyes widened. "He does?"

"He needs someone to work directly with him."

"Oh my God. That might mean I could work from Kentucky."

Her eyes glittered with happiness and the lure of her lush mouth was as strong as an aphrodisiac. He wondered about his strength, his endurance, if he really could paint her without touching her.

But his fears melted away when he remembered he couldn't watch her pregnancy. And now he knew she was going home to her mom and a job from Tucker.

She would not be around forever. His endurance didn't have to last a lifetime. Only a few weeks. He had nothing to worry about.

CHAPTER NINE

WHEN THEY ARRIVED at Antonio's country home the next day, everything had a different feel to it. They were no longer adversaries. They were partners in his plan to paint again. The feeling of being on even ground was heady stuff for Laura Beth. She'd always been second-best, plain Laura Beth. Today they were equals.

Standing in the foyer, she faced him with a smile. "So? Ready to go to the studio?"

"It's Sunday."

"I thought artists had to work while they were inspired. Do you want to lose your momentum?"

She could tell from the expression that flitted across his handsome face that he didn't. Still, he said, "How about lunch first?"

She caught his hand and tugged him in the direction of the back door that led to his studio. "How about work first?"

He laughed. "Wow. I have never known you to turn down food."

"I had a peanut-butter-and-jelly sandwich while you took that catnap on the plane."

She turned the knob on the ratty door of the cottage and it gave easily. Surprise almost had her turning to ask why he didn't lock the door, then she realized he was totally comfortable here in the Italian countryside. Which was probably part of why it drove him so crazy not to be able to paint. This was his sanctuary, and it was letting him down. Since his wife's death, everybody and everything seemed to be letting him down. She would not.

Pride billowed through her. She might make nothing else of her life, but helping him to paint again would be her crowning accomplishment. Even if she never told another soul, to protect his pride, she would know simple Laura Beth Matthews had done something wonderful.

They wound their way through the maze of old paint cans, broken furniture and fabrics to the last room. His studio.

Happy, she faced him with a smile. "So where do I sit? What do I do?"

He ran his hand down his face. "We just got off a plane. Give me a minute to adjust."

His hesitancy filled the air. He wanted this so much and he'd tried and failed before. She knew that trying again, he faced disappointment again.

She stepped back, giving him space. "Sure."

He glanced around, then rummaged through stacks of paper in the drawer of a metal desk so old it didn't even have accommodations for a computer. He pulled out two tablets. One was huge. The other was the size of a spiral notebook. He set the large pad of paper on the top of the desk, and opened the smaller one.

"We'll do sketches first."

"What do you want me to do?"

"First, I just need to warm up, get the feel of your features, the shape of your body."

She nodded eagerly.

"So, I'll sit here." He leaned his hip on the corner of the desk. "And you sit there." He pointed at a ladder-back chair about ten feet away.

She frowned. "There?"

"Yes. These are preliminaries. Warm-ups. Something to get me accustomed to your shapes."

Her gaze involuntarily rippled to the chaise near the windows. That would have been more comfortable. She wanted to sit there.

But he pointed at the ladder-back chair again.

She smiled hesitantly. Though she understood what he was saying, something really drew her to that chaise. Still, she sat on the ladder-back chair. Antonio picked up a simple number-two pencil.

"Really? A pencil? You're not going to use charcoal or chalk or anything cool like that?"

He sighed and dropped the tablet to his lap. "I'm warming up!"

She waved her hand. "Okay. Okay. Whatever."

By the time Antonio had her seated on the chair, his anxiety about drawing had shimmied away. Praying that she would stop talking and especially stop second-guessing his choices, he picked up his pencil and began sketching quickly, easily, hoping to capture at least five minutes of her sitting still.

When she wrinkled her nose, as if it was itchy, he stopped and stretched. He'd drawn small sketches of her eyes, her nose, her lips, her neck, her eyebrows, the wrinkle in her forehead, the side view of her hair looping across her temple and one sketch of her entire face.

"If you need to scratch your nose, scratch."

She pulled in a breath and rubbed her palm across her nose. "Thank God."

"What? You were sitting for…" He glanced at his watch. "Wow. Ten minutes. I guess you do deserve a break. For someone unaccustomed to posing, ten minutes is a long time."

She popped off the chair. Shook out all her limbs. "I know I've sat perfectly still for more than ten minutes at a time, but sitting still without anything to think about or do? That's hard."

"I'd actually hoped to break you in with five-minute increments."

"Meaning?"

"You'd sit for five minutes a few times in our first two settings, then ten minutes in our third and fifteen in our fourth…that kind of thing."

"So we're skipping a step?"

"Which could be good."

"Can I see what you've done?"

He handed her the tablet.

She smiled. "These are great."

"That's just me messing around until I get a good feel for drawing your features. Then we move on to sketches of what I think a painting of you should look like."

She beamed at him and everything inside him lit up. He told himself he was happy that she was enjoying the process, happy that he hadn't yet had an anxiety attack, and motioned her back to the chair.

"If you can keep doing ten-minute sessions, we'll do two more, then break for the day."

"You're only working a half hour?"

He laughed. "Yes. I'm not just indoctrinating you into the process. I'm easing myself in too."

She sat on the chair, straightened her spine and lifted her face. "Okay."

He sketched for ten minutes, gave her a break,

sketched for ten more, then they had lunch. Later, while she sat by the pool, he paid his dad a visit. He expected them to argue like two overemotional Italians about Constanzo stranding them in Barcelona. Instead, his father quietly apologized, told Antonio he was tired and retired to his room.

The next day, Laura Beth easily graduated to sitting for fifteen minutes at a time. The day after that, she had a bit of trouble with sitting for twenty minutes, but eventually got it.

He drew her face over and over and over again. He sketched her arms, her feet, the slope of her shoulder. Feeling the rhythm of those shapes in his hand as it flowed over the paper, he felt little bits of himself returning. But he didn't push. Fearing he'd tumble into bad territory, he didn't let himself feel. He simply put pencil to paper.

On Sunday, with Ricky and Eloise in Italy on the last leg of their honeymoon, he forced Laura Beth to take the day off to visit with them.

Monday morning, though, she arrived in his studio, bright and eager to begin.

Trembling with equal parts of anticipation and terror over the next step of the process, he busied himself with organizing his pencils as he said, "This week we're doing potential poses for the painting."

"So now I don't just have to sit still? I have to sit still a certain way."

He glanced up. Her eyes were bright. Her smile brilliant. Enthusiasm virtually vibrated from her body.

"Basically, yes."

Knowing how uncomfortable the ladder-back chair had been, he walked her to the wall of windows in the back of the room. He posed her feet, positioned her shoulders, placed her hands together at her stomach and strode back to the old metal desk to get his pad and pencil.

He worked for twenty minutes, trying again and again to make her come to life in a sketch, but failing. He knew what he wanted. That faraway look. And though he saw snatches of it in her eyes, it didn't stay and he couldn't catch it when it was only a glimpse.

With a sigh, he said, "Let's take a break."

"Wow. Was that a half hour already?"

"Twenty minutes. I can't seem to get what I want from this pose, so I figured we'd stop, give me a bit of rest and try again."

After a bathroom break and a few sips of water, Laura Beth was ready to go again. Antonio picked up his pencil and tablet. She positioned herself and Antonio started drawing. After only a few seconds, he said, "The light is wrong."

She deflated from her pose. "Bummer."

He shook his head. "It is a bummer, but we can come back to this tomorrow morning. Right now…" He glanced around. "Let's try one with you sitting on the chaise."

She walked over and sat down. Without waiting for instructions, she angled herself on the chair with her back to him, then looked over her shoulder at him.

The vivid image of her lying wrapped in the towel on her bed popped into his head, quickly followed by the pose he'd so desperately wanted to paint. Her wrapped in silk, one shoulder and her entire back bare, the swell of her hip peeking out at him, her face a study of innocence.

His finger itched to capture that. But he was sure the urge was a leftover of an aberration. Watching her at the gallery, he'd envisioned several compelling poses, expressions, little bits of humanity that would result in a painting every bit as compelling. He did not need to go *there*.

"That's not how I want you."

"Okay."

"Let's try this." He wasn't entirely sure how to position her. He had facial expressions in his mind. Images of her hair falling just the right way. And he couldn't seem to get it right as he shifted her from one side to another, one pose to another.

"Okay. How about this? Lie down and pretend you're daydreaming."

"Oh! I get to lie down!"

He stopped in midstep toward the metal desk and faced her. "If you're tired or anything, I don't want you to overdo."

She stretched out on the sofa. "I'm fine."

Her inelegant movement struck a chord in him again and he eagerly grabbed the notebook. That was part of the essence he was trying to grasp. Beautiful yet impish. Troubled but still hopeful. With the image fresh in his mind, he began sketching. But after ten minutes he realized that pose didn't work either.

Neither surprised nor disappointed—today was all about trying and failing—he gave her a break, then sat her on a chair.

Backing away from her, he said, "Think deep thoughts."

Her face scrunched. "How deep?"

"I don't know." Remembering the feelings he'd had in the gallery and their subsequent conversation, he said, "Think about going home."

She nodded, and he watched the change come to her

eyes. Almost a sadness. Something tweaked inside him. But he didn't say anything. Though he wanted to comfort her, they weren't supposed to become friends from this. He wanted to paint her. She wanted to go home.

It made him sad. Almost angry. But he got the best sketches of the day.

After that they stopped for lunch. Rosina had prepared salads and bread, but Laura Beth skipped the bread, insisting she could *feel* herself getting fat.

He watched her single out and then dig in to her tomatoes with gusto and had to stifle a laugh. Feeling light and airy because he counted that morning as a success, he didn't want to upset her in any way, shape or form. But the look in her eyes as he'd sketched her haunted him.

Casually, as if it were the most natural question in the world, he asked, "Do you not want to go home?"

Her head popped up. Her gaze swung to his. "I need to go home."

"There's a wide gulf between need and want."

"I need my mother. Aside from Tucker and Olivia's kids, I've never been around a baby. And I can't really count Tucker and Olivia's kids because I've never changed their diapers, never fed one of them and most certainly never walked the floor."

"Ah. I get it. You need your mother's assistance."

"More her advice…her knowledge. Which means, since I need her so much, I *want* to go home."

He laughed. "That's convoluted at best."

She shrugged. "It is what it is."

But the faraway, sad expression came to her eyes again. He should have yearned to grab his pencil. Instead, that odd something tweaked inside him again.

Only this time, he recognized it. It wasn't a worry that they would get close. He hated to see her sad.

"What if you got a nanny?"

She gaped at him for a few seconds, then laughed out loud. "Right. I can't even afford an apartment. Hell, Tucker hasn't officially offered me a job yet, and you want me to hire a nanny?"

"But if he does offer you a job with a good enough salary, it would mean you could live where you want. That you wouldn't have to go back to a small town that clearly makes you sad."

"The town doesn't make me sad. I told you before. I want my child to be raised there."

He frowned. "So what makes you sad?"

Laura Beth fumbled with her napkin. For fifty cents she'd tell him the truth. She'd look him right in the eye and say, "I like being with you. I like the person I am with you. And I am going to be sad when I leave because I know I'll only ever see you at parties where we'll be polite like strangers."

But then he'd draw back. Then he wouldn't paint her. He might even put her in Constanzo's plane and ship her home so he didn't have to deal with her feelings.

So she'd handle them alone.

"I think it's just hormones."

"Ah." He nodded. "I seem to recall hearing a bit about them from Tucker when Olivia was pregnant."

And that was it. He totally believed her. He didn't even like her enough to say, "Are you sure?" He didn't dig deeper. Proof, again, that he didn't have the same kinds of feelings for her that she had for him.

In bed that night, she cautioned herself about getting so close to him—wouldn't let herself pretend there was any chance they'd be together—and the next morning she forced herself to be as chipper and happy as any woman posing for a portrait should be. She couldn't have him forever, but that didn't mean she couldn't enjoy what she had now. In fact, a wise woman would accept what she could get and make memories.

After breakfast, Antonio took her outside. She'd asked him a million times if there was anything special he wanted her to wear and every time he'd said, "Your jeans are fine."

But his attempts at capturing an outside pose failed. When the next day's poses also resulted in balled-up paper and strings of curses in Italian, Laura Beth had to hide several winces. On Friday, when his temper appeared—a real, live temper that went beyond curses and balled-up paper and resulted in explosions and tablets tossed into the trash—fear trembled through her.

Not fear of Antonio. She knew he would never hurt her. His anger was never directed at her, but always at himself. His lost focus. His inability to capture what he wanted. She also saw his volatility as part of his larger-than-life personality, very much like his dad's. What scared her was that he might quit trying and ask her to leave.

The very thought caused her chest to tighten. So Saturday after breakfast she suggested she meet him in the studio. He frowned and asked why, but she only smiled and raced off.

She styled her hair as it had been the night of the gallery opening, put on makeup and slipped into the black dress and the high heels Constanzo had bought her.

When she walked into the studio, Antonio had his back to her. She straightened her shoulders, lifted her chin and sashayed over to the wall of windows.

When he saw her, Antonio's face fell. He gaped at her for a good twenty seconds, then grabbed the tablet. Not knowing if the lighting was good or bad, she simply stood there. She thought deep thoughts, trying to get that faraway look he always talked about catching. She knew that the sooner the painting was done, the sooner she'd be going home, but she didn't care that dressing in the way that had inspired him would result in her going home. She longed to help him. This wasn't just about her doing something important with her life anymore. This was about him. About wanting him to get his life back.

And if the way he frantically scribbled was any indication, she was succeeding. Finally giving her man what he needed.

Her man.

She struggled with the urge to close her eyes. He was her man. She could feel it in her bones. And she was his muse. But he would let her go. Because he believed he'd had his woman, the love of his life, and even though Gisella was gone, he didn't want another love.

What she felt for him was pointless.

Antonio put down his pencil forty minutes later, belatedly realizing he'd made her stand stiff and silent way beyond her limitations.

"I'm sorry, *cara*."

She shook her shoulders loose, then smiled. "It's fine. Did you get what you wanted?"

"Yes." The desire to kiss her rose strong and sure. It wasn't just her pretty face and her bright personality that drew him. Her unselfish gestures never ceased to amaze him. For almost an hour, she'd stood stiff and straight, barely blinking. Even more, though, she'd realized what he needed when he didn't. The dress, the hair, even the shoes had brought back the feelings he'd had in the gallery, and his artistic instincts hadn't merely appeared. They'd jumped to full-blown life.

Because she'd made all the connections he couldn't seem to.

Still, he fought the urge to kiss her by turning away, puttering with his tablets, pretending interest in old sketches that had no value now that he'd found what he wanted. "Thank you for thinking of the dress."

She displayed her spike heels. "And let's not forget the shoes and hair."

She said it lightly, but an undercurrent of melancholy ran through her voice. All of this was about him. Nothing they'd done in the past ten days helped her. She still had her troubles.

He walked over and caught her hands. Fear of getting too close, of longing to kiss her, had to be shoved aside. He owed her. "You look so pretty. Let me take you to lunch."

She shook her head. "Nah. You don't have to."

"I insist. Give me ten minutes to clean up."

"It's okay. There's no need to thank me."

He smiled. "I'll let you drive."

Her eyes widened. "Do you have a Jag?"

"I have a Lamborghini."

"Oh, dear God." She pressed her hand to her chest. "How can I turn *that* down?"

He motioned for her to precede him out of the studio and up the cobblestone path, then headed to his room to change. Considering her attire, he slid into beige slacks and a short-sleeved white shirt, which he left open at the throat.

When she saw his car, she squealed with delight and

raced to get behind the wheel. He tossed the keys at her. She caught them like a left fielder for the Yankees. The engine rumbled to life and she shifted into reverse to get them out of the garage, then shoved the pedal to the floor when they reached the road.

The noise from the wind swirling around the open roof prevented conversation, so he pointed to give her directions to the nearest small town. He motioned with his hand to let her know she needed to slow down as they drew closer.

They entered the village and their speed decreased. The noise of the wind diminished. He heard the appreciative sigh that told him she was pleased with his choice of village, with its cobblestone streets, old houses, street vendors and sidewalk cafés.

"Park here."

She pulled the car into a little space. They both got out and he directed her to walk to the right.

The way she looked at his little town was like nothing he'd ever seen before. Her lips kicked upward into a smile of pure joy, but not like a person surprised by what she saw. More like a woman who'd found a place she loved.

Mesmerized by her excitement, he caught her hand and led her down the street to the outdoor seating of his favorite local restaurant.

They ordered salads and once again she refused bread. He shook his head. "You are supposed to gain weight."

"Yeah, but I'm not supposed to turn into a tub of lard."

He laughed. "The way you talk reminds me of my childhood."

Her gaze rose to meet his. "Really?"

"Yes. Everybody I know either speaks Italian or they're a bigwig in the art world or in one of Dad's former companies. You speak like a normal person."

"I am a normal person."

"And most of my foster parents were normal."

Her eyes softened. "Did you have a rough time?"

He shook his head. "Tucker had a rough time. I think that's because he was actually in New York City. I was in a quiet city in Pennsylvania. I had a bit of trouble with being angry about not knowing my dad, but my foster parents were always simple, normal people with big hearts."

She said, "Hmm," then cocked her head. "Pennsylvania's not so different from Kentucky."

He chuckled. "You have a twang that Pennsylvanians don't."

She frowned. "Hey, I worked really hard to get rid of that twang."

"And you've mostly succeeded."

Laughing, Laura Beth glanced across the table at Antonio. The blue sky smiled down on them. A light breeze kept everything cool. The hum of life, of street vendors, cars and chatting passersby, filled the place with life and energy. She totally understood why Tucker and Olivia spent several months a year in Italy. If she could, she would, too. But in a few days she'd be going home. Back to her blue-collar roots. Back where she belonged.

Emotion clogged her throat. She wouldn't just miss Antonio. She would miss his world. Italy. Art. Interesting people. Sun that warmed everything.

Still, she swallowed back her feelings. She'd already decided her future was in her small town with her parents. Because she loved that world, too. She loved crisp autumns. Sleigh rides and skating in the winter. The love of people she knew. A quiet, humble place to raise a child.

It just seemed so unfair that she had to choose. But, really, she didn't have a choice. She was broke. Longing to live in two worlds was the last resort of a foolish woman. And she knew it was time to get sensible. The best way to do that would be to take the focus of this conversation off herself and get it back on him.

"Tell me more about your childhood." Changing her mind, she waved her hand to stop his response. "No. Tell me about Constanzo finding you. I've only ever heard bits and pieces of that story from Olivia. I'd love to hear it from your perspective."

He grinned sheepishly and glanced down at his empty salad plate. A waitress strolled over and said something in Italian before she poured him a second glass of wine and took his empty plate.

He sucked in a breath. "Imagine being exactly where you are right now financially, taking your last pennies and getting on a plane to another continent and literally swapping a painting every month for your rent."

She sighed dreamily. "It sounds romantic."

"It was terrifying."

"Yes, but at least you had something to barter. You had paintings that your landlord obviously wanted."

He sniffed a laugh. "Don't think he was being altruistic. I'm sure he's made a bundle off me."

"Maybe. But you still had something to trade."

"Right. After I bought the canvases and paint." He shook his head. "I was always scrambling for odd jobs, in a country I didn't know, as I learned to speak the language."

The breeze lifted the hair around his shoulders and

she saw the tip of the webbed wing of his dragon tattoo, the sexy contrast to the quiet, calm man before her. Totally captivated by his smooth voice and his cool sophistication in the white shirt that accented his olive skin, she put her elbow on the table and her chin on her fist. "So what happened?"

He lifted his wineglass. "Constanzo bartered Tucker into paving the way for us to meet."

"So he'd already found you?"

Antonio nodded. "Yes. But he was clumsy about it. He'd chased my mom out of his office when she told him she was pregnant and she'd disappeared, gone to America without even telling her family where she was going. Humiliated, she clearly didn't want anyone to find her." He swirled the wine in his glass. "Her family didn't even know I existed. But Constanzo knew that somewhere in the world was a child he'd rejected and he knew our getting to know each other wasn't going to be easy."

"Wow."

"So Constanzo enlisted Tucker's help, but it was actually Olivia who brought me into the fold."

"I don't understand."

"Tucker is like a bull in a china shop. Very much like my dad. Olivia appealed to me as a person. We connected immediately."

She smiled. She could see Olivia and Antonio connecting. She saw signs of their closeness every time they were together. Until he'd stopped painting, they'd been totally in sync about his career. They connected like friends, not romantically, the way Laura Beth was drawn to him. But that was probably why it had been so easy for Antonio and Olivia. They were friends only, while she and Antonio had an attraction flipping back and forth between them, a longing to be close that actually somehow kept them separated.

"So how did they spring it on you that you were the long-lost son of a billionaire?"

"My cousin Maria had apparently figured everything out." He laughed. "Maria makes bulls in china shops look tame. So rather than risk that she'd bulldoze the information into a conversation, they told me at my first showing here in Italy."

She winced. "Yikes."

"It was weird. But Constanzo had been involved in the preparations for the showing right from the beginning as backer. So I'd gotten to know him a bit, and when they told me he was my dad, instead of that resulting in confusion, it just sort of pulled everything together."

The warm breeze ruffled past again, drawing her gaze to the square, the tourists and street vendors. "That's nice."

"What about you?"

Her gaze snapped over to his. Asking about his dad was supposed to keep the conversation off her. Now, here he was, bringing it back to her again. "Me?"

"Any odd stories in your life?"

"Unless you count the story of me getting pregnant, my life has been simple. Uncomplicated." She shrugged. "Which is why I'm simple, silly Laura Beth."

"Have you ever thought that being simple, being honest, being kind is a good thing?"

Her breath stuttered into her lungs. This was why she was falling head over heels in love with him. He didn't just like her as she was. He made her feel that who she was was more than enough. It was special. And she was so hungry to be special that she gobbled up his compliments like gelato.

"I used to."

"You should start believing it again." He took her hand and she froze. The way he touched her always sent a zing of excitement through her, but it also always felt right. Natural. As if the two of them had been created to touch and love and talk.

"To me, you are wonderful."

If she still had a sliver of her heart left, he took it with those words. And the horrible truth hit her. She wasn't falling in love with Antonio. She was already totally gone. So in love with him that when she had to leave, her heart would dissolve into a puddle of sadness.

CHAPTER TEN

GETTING READY FOR bed that night, she once again forced herself to face reality. She truly loved Antonio, and she believed he loved her too. Not the head-over-heels way she loved him, or the way he'd loved Gisella, but in a quieter, gentler way.

But he didn't *want* to love her. She saw the hesitation in his eyes every time he pulled his hands back, stepped away from her, turned away rather than kiss her. His wife might be dead, but she was very much alive in Antonio's heart. If he loved Laura Beth, and she believed he did, it wouldn't be the same way Tucker adored Olivia or Ricky worshipped Eloise. It would be a quiet, simple, you-are-second-best kind of love.

She let that realization wash over her because it would dictate every decision she made from now until she boarded a plane and left him…left this beautiful place.

Knowing that he had feelings for her, she could push him to admit them. She could promise him the one thing he truly wanted—his ability to paint. She could be his muse forever.

She would win him. Win a place in his life.

But even if he asked her to marry him, she would always be second-best.

Was winning the object of her love, getting to be with the man she loved, worth never being in first place in anyone's life?

She didn't know. Right now, just the thought of leaving him, or only seeing him at friends' functions, where he'd be distantly polite to her, shattered her heart. She wasn't even sure she could walk away. As much as she needed her mom's help, she also needed Antonio. She needed to hear him say she was special. She needed the feeling of purpose he'd inspired in her.

But she also needed to be someone's one true love.

And Antonio had had his one true love.

Antonio refused to work on Sunday, so it was Monday morning before they headed to the studio again. Knowing they would be working, she'd worn the black dress and spike heels, wound her hair into the fancy hairdo and put on makeup.

He raced down the cobblestone path. "Today is the day I get you on canvas."

She laughed. "Really? All in one day?"

"I'll do a slight pencil drawing today and from here on out you won't need to pose every day, just when I want to be reminded of something."

"Sounds good."

It really didn't sound good. It sounded like the beginning of the end. Still, she kept up the happy facade as he chose canvas, found pencils and went to work.

But he cursed at his first attempts to sketch her. He took digital pictures and studied the light, the angle of her head, shoulders and torso. But nothing pleased him. By noon, he was annoyed with himself, and they quit for the day.

Tuesday, he got angry. He'd drawn plenty of versions

of her, had captured the look he wanted in his initial drawings, but none of the sketches on canvas caught the look he wanted to show the world.

On Wednesday, she tried talking. So what if her face was moving? He wasn't getting anything he liked anyway. And when she talked, she usually calmed him or inspired him. But that day it didn't help.

As he ran an eraser over the shadowy pencil lines he'd made, her purpose shivered through her. The one thing she really wanted out of life—the one memory she wanted to hold in her heart to prove her time had meant something—was to pull him out of his anger, his funk, and get him painting again, and she was failing.

So she asked about Constanzo and let Antonio relax as he talked about his dad, about the success of his first showing and his rapid rise in the world of art. But he still sighed heavily and tossed that morning's canvas out the back door as if it were trash.

She wondered if sweet, wonderful Gisella had ever seen his little fits of temper, and had to hold back a gasp. They'd never spoken about his wife! They'd never even brushed against the real reason he didn't paint. And she suddenly saw the mistake in that. By ignoring that they were, in effect, trying to put a bandage on an open wound. She'd brought him this far by being someone he wanted to paint, but what if that was only half the battle? What if he needed to talk out some of his pain? What if he needed to face the sadness inside him before he could actually use his talent to the fullest?

As he set another canvas on the easel, she swallowed. Sucked in a breath. Prayed for strength. And finally said, "So is this what happened when you stopped painting?"

He peered over. "Excuse me?"

"Did you try canvas after canvas and toss them aside?"

He bristled. "Yes."

"So tell me about it."

"No."

She sighed. "Look, I get it that you can't paint because you lost the love of your life. I just lost a boyfriend who didn't really like me and it hurt like hell. But you lost the love of your life. You need to address that."

His expression shifted from angry to confused. Twice, he opened his mouth to say something. Twice, he stopped himself.

"What?"

He licked his lips and turned away. "Nothing."

Purpose rattled through her again. She needed to get him to admit he'd quit painting because without his wife his art had no meaning. He needed to say the words. Needed those words to come out into the open so he could face them. "It's not nothing. It's *something*. Tell me."

"I don't want to talk about it."

"Look, this…me posing for you…is all about you getting your mojo back. So we've hit an impasse." She glanced down at her black dress and heels, then smiled up at him. "I helped you through the last one by recreating the look that inspired you. Now I'm sensing that it's your wife—your love for your wife—that's holding you back. I don't think I'm wrong. You need to talk about it."

He tossed his pencil to the metal desk, massaged his forehead, then laughed slightly. "No."

A minute went by in complete silence, but eventually he picked up a pencil and began drawing a light outline on the canvas.

Desperation filled her, but so did a realization. In

falling for him so quickly, she'd forgotten his real pain. Maybe the first move was actually hers. "I don't think I ever told you I was sorry."

He peeked away from his work, across the room at her. "For what?"

"That you lost your wife." She paused a second. Though forcing him to talk about his wife was the right thing to do, it hurt. Gisella was the reason he would never love her. And she gave herself a space of time to acknowledge that pain before she said, "She was beautiful."

He turned his attention back to the canvas. "Yes. She was."

Laura Beth swallowed hard. "And special."

He said nothing.

"Please. I think you need to talk about her."

"No."

"My gram told me one of the hardest things about losing my pap was that after a few weeks people stopped talking about him. She longed to remember him, to keep his memory alive, and people seemed to forget him."

"Laura Beth, please. That's enough."

"I just want you to know that you can talk about her with me."

He stepped away from the canvas, his spine stiff, his eyes narrow. Irritation vibrated from him across the room to her. "Dear God! Will you just let it drop?"

She snapped her mouth shut. She knew he might not be eager to talk about Gisella, but she hadn't expected him to get angry. "I'm sorry. I just desperately want this for you. I want you to be able to paint again."

Antonio's fingers tightened on his pencil. He realized she was trying to help him relax by what she considered to be a logical method, but she had no way of knowing her comments about his wife were actually doing more harm than good.

Still, it wasn't her fault. No one knew the real story, his real pain, and though he would die before he would admit his failings, he could at least let Laura Beth know she wasn't at fault.

"Look, my wife wasn't exactly what everyone thought."

"Okay."

Again a soft word filled with regret. He shifted a bit, putting himself solidly behind the canvas. He hated the self-loathing in her voice. Hated that he was responsible for it. He might not be able to tell her the whole story, but he could tiptoe around enough facts that she'd stop feeling bad.

"I'm not angry with you. I've simply never spoken about my wife with anyone."

"I still think you should."

He sniffed a laugh. "Honestly, *carissima*, I don't know what I'd say."

"Why don't you just tell me the truth?"

The truth would probably scandalize her. But he suddenly noticed that his pencil was moving with easy efficiency. The image he captured was perfect. His vision. Exactly what he wanted.

He didn't know if it was the pose or the distraction of talking or even the power of the topic, but he was working…effortlessly. And he couldn't break the spell, ruin the moment or lose the opportunity.

"I wish I could tell you the truth." As the words spilled out and the picture before him began to take shape, something inside his chest loosened. A weird kind of excitement nudged his heart, and he wondered if she was right. Did he need to talk about his wife to let his anger with her go?

His pencil paused. He glanced over at Laura Beth. He might need to talk, but was Laura Beth—was anyone—ready to hear what he had to say? "The story of my marriage is not a happy one."

She frowned and the look he'd been trying to capture flitted over her features, filled her eyes. A longing so intense it shifted every muscle in her face, darkened her eyes.

His pencil began to move again, feverishly, desperate to get that expression.

"You weren't happy?"

"Is anybody ever really happy?"

"Don't talk in abstracts when you know the truth. Olivia and Tucker are happy. Content. Eloise and Ricky are happy. You know happy. You know what it looks like. So you know if you were happy or not."

Absorbed in his work, more grateful that he was succeeding than antsy about the conversation, he said, "Then we were not."

"Then I'm sorry." She waited a beat before she said, "Want to tell me what happened?"

As his pencil captured the fine details that made Laura Beth who she was, he weighed his options. Sunlight pouring in from the wall of windows gave the quiet room the feel of a sacred space. A time and place he could be honest. Having been left by the father of her child, if anyone could understand his situation, it would be Laura Beth.

And if telling her the truth was what he needed to do to rid himself of the demons that tormented him, then so be it.

He cut right to the chase, didn't mince words, but

was as honest, as open, as she'd asked him to be. "My wife ran around on me and aborted my child."

The words that sounded so simple, so reasonable, in his head leveled him. His wife had gotten rid of his baby. Made a mockery of his naive love for her. Made him a fool. And now the words were out in the open, hanging on the air.

Behind the canvas, he squeezed his eyes shut, ran his angry fingers along his forehead. What was he doing?

He heard a soft swish, then saw Laura Beth's long legs approaching before she appeared at his side.

"I am so sorry."

A piece of her dark hair had fallen loose from its pins and framed her face. Her green eyes filled with sadness.

"I shouldn't have told you."

"What? That your marriage was a mess?"

"That my marriage was a lie. And I was a fool."

She stepped closer, examining his face. "All this time, I thought you were mourning her." She shook her head as if confused. "Everybody thought you'd been so sad these past years because you mourned her."

"Not her, my child. To the world she was an icon. But I lived the truth. She was a narcissist, who did everything she did not out of love or compassion but to make herself look important." He caught Laura Beth's gaze. "For two years I've been trapped. I couldn't tell the world who or what she was and yet I couldn't live the lie."

Her face softened. "Oh, Antonio."

Turning away from her, he grabbed a cloth and wiped his hands.

"You should talk about this with Olivia. She knows all about being forced to live a lie."

He shook his head. "I don't really want anyone to know."

"I know."

He sniffed a laugh.

"So maybe, since you started opening up, you should keep going." She paused, waited for him to look at her. "Get it off your shoulders."

Her honest eyes beckoned. The feeling of something loosening in his chest shuddered through him again and he knew she was right. He'd started the story. He needed to finish it.

"A year after we were married, she scheduled a trip for her charity. I'd lost her itinerary, so I went into her computer to find it and what I found was an identical itinerary for a man. She had an explanation, of course, so I felt foolish for accusing her."

He walked away from the easel. "Dear God, she held that first accusation over my head every time I questioned something she said or did. She'd remind me of how bad I felt over that mistake and I'd back off. For months, I believed lie after lie. Then she began to get careless. Her lies weren't as tight. Newspaper pictures of her with one man became commonplace. I saw the smiles that passed between them. I *saw* the intimacy. Until eventually I got so angry I went through the documents in her computer in earnest and that's when I found the abortion."

Laura Beth squeezed her eyes shut. "I'm so sorry, Antonio."

"She denied it. But I told her I had seen the appointment on her calendar, the check that paid the clinic. She told me that her life was her charity and she didn't want any time taken away from that for any reason. She said she wasn't cut out to be a mom. I exploded and told her

I wanted to be a dad and she laughed. That's when I knew our marriage was over." He tossed a rag to the table. "I don't believe she ever loved anyone as much as she loved herself. The fact that she didn't even give me an option with our child proved she never thought beyond herself."

"I'm so sorry."

"You needn't be. She taught me some valuable lessons. People change. Love doesn't last." He sniffed a laugh. "Trust no one."

The room grew quiet. Antonio heard the click of her heels again. When he turned she was right behind him.

"She didn't deserve you."

He sniffed a laugh.

"I'm serious."

"I have my faults."

"Oh, don't I know it. But I still think you're special." She caught his gaze. "Wonderful."

The magnetic pull of her innocent green eyes drew him to her. An inch. Then two. Then his hands were close enough that he could lay them on her warm shoulders. His mouth was close enough that he could touch his lips to hers.

As if thought gave birth to action, he closed the distance between them and brushed his lips across hers. Laura Beth edged closer too. Her lips were warm and sweet. The way she kissed him, answering the moves of his mouth slowly, hesitantly, then completely, spoke of submission. Honesty. A change in the way she felt about him, the way she related to him. She was taking the step that would shift them from friends to so much more.

He slid his tongue along the seam of her lips and when she opened to him he deepened the kiss.

CHAPTER ELEVEN

LAURA BETH SURRENDERED to the urgent prodding of Antonio's mouth. Desperate, shivering with need, she pressed into him as he pulled her closer.

He didn't mourn his wife.

He did want her.

She could be the love of his life.

Except he didn't trust.

The cell phone in his pocket began to chime out a happy beat. Antonio pulled away. Their gazes caught and held.

The phone rang again.

Antonio quietly said, "That ringtone is Bernice, my father's assistant. She never calls unless it's an emergency."

Laura Beth whispered, "You should take it."

As if in a trance, he nodded, retrieved the phone from his pocket and clicked the button to answer it. "Bernice? What's up?"

Because he'd put his phone on speaker, the voice of Constanzo's assistant erupted in the room. "Oh, Antonio! It's awful! Just awful!"

Laura Beth walked a few feet away. Her head spun—the truth about his life, his marriage, had shaken her to the core. It gave her a crazy kind of hope, even as it dashed her hopes. How could she expect to build a life with a man who couldn't trust?

Antonio said, "Hey. Calm down. Whatever my dad did, we can fix it."

"This isn't about a mistake." A sob escaped. "The ambulance just left. Your dad is on his way to the hospital. They think he had a heart attack."

Antonio stumbled to the chaise and collapsed on it. "A heart attack?"

Laura Beth gasped. "Oh, my God." All her other thoughts and troubles flitted away in a surge of worry about Constanzo.

"Yes! Hurry! Get to the hospital!"

He disconnected the call as Laura Beth walked to the door. "You give me directions and I'll drive."

Antonio raced out of the studio toward the house for keys. "*I'll* drive."

She didn't follow him, but ran to the garage. In less than a minute, Antonio joined her with his car keys. He jumped into the Lamborghini and Laura Beth climbed in too.

As he sped along the winding roads of the hills between his country house and Bogodehra, she wasn't sure it was wise for him to drive. But she was as desperate to get to the hospital as he was, and simply held onto the dashboard for support as they raced to the city.

When they finally arrived at the stucco building with loops of arches and fancy pillars, they jumped out and dashed inside.

Laura Beth's gaze winged from side to side as she took in the surroundings that were both familiar and unfamiliar. Department names were in Italian, but most of the words were close enough to English that she could translate. Still, the chatter of doctors, nurses, patients and patients' families in the area best described by an American as the emergency room was in Italian. Even Antonio spoke Italian when he reached a nurse's station.

Using the universal language of pointing, the nurse obviously told him to have a seat.

He sighed and faced Laura Beth. "We can't see him."

She caught his arm frantically. "We can't?"

He squeezed his eyes shut and Laura Beth realized she wasn't helping by panicking.

"They haven't yet gotten the word that he's stable."

Her heart dipped. Fear crept into her limbs and froze them. It was impossible for her to picture an event for one of Tucker and Olivia's kids without big, boisterous Constanzo Bartulocci, the man everyone thought of like a favorite uncle.

If she was this upset about Constanzo, she couldn't imagine Antonio's fright. Constanzo was his *father*. If her father was the one in this hospital right now, she'd be a basket case.

She tugged lightly on his arm and got him to a plastic seat. As if in a daze, he lowered himself to the chair. She sat beside him, but took his hand, keeping the connection, so he'd know he wasn't alone.

"My father and I haven't really spoken since we got back from Barcelona. When I did stop by, he said he was sorry for stranding us, but didn't want to talk about anything else. I never went over after that."

She smiled weakly, acknowledging that. "We've been busy."

He put his head back and rubbed his hand across his mouth. "I should have gone to see him again. I should have forced him to talk about that fight, or at least let him know I wasn't angry." He sighed. "Why are we always squabbling?"

She squeezed his hand and again her sense of purpose, of destiny, with Antonio filled her. All she had to do was listen to the easy way he confided in her, talked about such personal things, to know that he trusted her. He might not realize it, but she did.

"It's how you show love."

He sniffed a laugh. "Right. Either that or he hates me."

That admission further bolstered her belief that there was more between them than friendship, more between them than a few kisses. And she knew she was the person to help him through this crisis.

"He doesn't hate you. If he did, he wouldn't meddle."

Antonio shut his eyes. "He always meddles."

"Yeah, but I think his intentions are good. I'm sure Tucker and Olivia were glad he forced them to come to Italy together to find you."

He sniffed a laugh. "Such a matchmaker and a do-gooder."

"Lots of people would be glad their dad looks for ways to help other people."

"I am. Most days I'm proud of him." He sighed and closed his eyes. "I wish I'd told him that."

She tightened her hold on his hand. "I'm sure he knows."

"By my yelling at him?"

"By the fact that you're honest with each other." She thought of her parents back in Kentucky. "I wish I could be so open with my parents."

He turned his head and studied her. "You're not?"

"I haven't yet told them I'm pregnant." She shrugged. "I'm afraid of their reaction. I don't think you and Constanzo hold important things back. Even if you do sometimes get loud when you talk."

Antonio's eyes softened. "Have you even called your parents?"

Knowing the distraction of a different topic might be good for him, she said, "Yes. Once. I let them know I was here in Italy."

"Why haven't you told them?"

"I guess deep down I'm afraid of what they'll say. They'd wanted me to become a doctor or a lawyer and start a practice in our small town." She sighed. "But I wanted something more."

"Something more?"

Knowing she was doing a good job of keeping Antonio occupied, she decided to be honest, to continue the conversation that held his nerves at bay. "That's the bad part. I couldn't even give them a description of what I wanted. All I could tell them was I had this feeling in my soul that I was meant to do something wonderful with my life."

He winced. "But you couldn't tell them what."

"No. And now I'm returning educated but not employable." She shook her head.

"Hey, Olivia says Tucker has a job for you."

"But what if he doesn't? There aren't a lot of jobs for IT people in Starlight, Kentucky. So I'll end up being somebody's glorified secretary. I'll be coming back a failure and pregnant."

His gaze slowly met hers. "Some people would consider a child a blessing."

She swallowed. Caught in the fierce light in his dark eyes, she could almost read his thoughts. He had lost a child because his wife hadn't thought beyond her own needs. Antonio himself was born to an unmarried mother, the product of the same kind of mistake Laura

Beth had made. It was important that Antonio know she did not consider her baby a mistake.

"My child is a blessing. I don't know why I got pregnant, but I believe in destiny. This little boy or girl has a purpose."

"What if his or her purpose is only to sweep streets?"

She laughed. "Destiny is about more than a job."

"You should tell that to yourself some time."

She frowned.

"You're so concerned that without a law degree or medical license your parents will consider you're a failure. What if your destiny is to be the mother of the surgeon who makes the next great medical advancement or the architect who builds the next Sistine Chapel? What if your destiny is simply to be this child's mom?"

As she thought about that, a smile bloomed. "I get it."

"And even if his destiny isn't to be great—even if his destiny is to sweep streets—he's still important."

She squeezed Antonio's hand. "I know. All along there's been something inside me that happily responded to the idea of raising a child. I won't let him down."

Antonio ran his free hand down his face again. Though the conversation had distracted him for a few minutes, his nervousness had returned.

A doctor in green scrubs walked to the nurse's station. The same nurse who'd relegated Antonio to a plastic seat pointed at him again. The doctor walked over.

Still clinging to Laura Beth's hand, Antonio rose.

The doctor began to speak in Italian. Antonio quickly cut him off. "English for my friend?"

The doctor nodded. "My English not perfect." He

smiled at Laura Beth. "But good enough. Your father's heart attack was mild, but we'll be running some tests. If all goes well, in a few days he will go home with medicine."

"If all doesn't go well?"

"Probably a bypass." The doctor smiled. "And a diet."

Antonio shook his head. He said, "Lucky old coot," but Laura Beth could feel the tension draining from him. "Can we see him?"

Making some notes on a chart, the doctor said, "Yes. I'm sure it will be a few minutes before he's wheeled out for testing."

Laura Beth and Antonio walked to Constanzo's cubicle hand in hand. Even before they reached it, they could hear the rumble of Constanzo's deep voice as he barked out complaints that his bed was too hard and he wanted a sandwich.

Pushing open the privacy curtain, Antonio said, "Too many sandwiches are what got you here."

As if glad for the reprieve, the nurses scrambled out of the cubicle.

Constanzo's eyes lit. "Laura Beth," he said, turning his pleading gaze on her, "I almost died. Tell my son to be kind to me."

She laughed, but the oddest feelings poured through her. In what should be a very private moment between a father and son, she didn't feel out of place. In fact, she felt as if she belonged here. But more than that, it felt right, perfect, that Antonio held her hand. Turned to her for comfort. Gave her advice when she tried to distract him. Liked her.

Her heart stumbled a bit as he released her hand and walked to the head of Constanzo's bed. Even though neither of them had said it, she and Antonio loved each other. Not in the way they'd loved Bruce or Gisella. But in a deep, profound way.

She was the real love of his life and he was hers.

And as soon as Constanzo was better, she would prove it to him.

With Constanzo safe in the hospital, his private doctors on the scene and a battery of tests ordered, Antonio's stress level fell. By the time they left the hospital, the sun had set. The air had cooled, but not so much that they had to put the Lamborghini's top up. He and Laura Beth didn't talk, but they didn't need to. She'd pushed him to tell the truth about Gisella and he'd forced her to admit why she'd really run to Italy. She might want to return to Starlight to raise her child, but she wasn't looking forward to the conversation she had to have with her parents. She didn't want to return to her hometown a failure.

Still, they were both on the road to recovery in their respective life crises. Now they could get on with their lives.

Already he felt strong again. Having learned his lessons about weakness, about letting anyone get too close, he'd never go through that kind of pain again. Just as Laura Beth would never again let herself be taken in by a man. She'd raise her child in her hometown and be happy.

He could picture it. He could see her in a big house with a homey kitchen and a yard full of green grass for a growing child. He smiled at the vision, but his smile quickly faded. He should have a three-year-old right now. A toddler to teach and dote on. Someone to make Constanzo smile. Someone who might grow up to be a garbageman or doctor. It wouldn't matter. He would have been Antonio's heart.

The Lamborghini roared up the driveway and, filled with indescribable pain, Antonio drove it into the garage. He and Laura Beth piled out unceremoniously. Though it was late, Rosina met them at the door to the kitchen.

"How is Mr. Constanzo?"

"He's fine."

Antonio's usually calm and collected housekeeper all but collapsed with relief.

His eyes narrowed as he directed her back into the kitchen. Her reaction had been more than a little extreme and he almost cursed the stupidity, the fruitlessness of his life. Servants who got involved in their lives like family—because they saw more of their household staff than the real world. Money. Talent. Fame. None of it mattered! He wanted his child.

"I will make sandwiches and you will tell me everything?"

He almost told her he wasn't hungry. He wanted to be alone. To lick his wounds. To roar with anger. But a glance at Laura Beth reminded him he had responsibilities. Not just to feed his probably starving guest, but to his staff. Rosina wanted information. He needed to give it to her.

"Sandwiches would be good."

Laura Beth took the stool beside his at the center island. As Rosina cut bread and assembled cold cuts, they told her everything the doctors had said. Reassured, and her job done, Rosina shuffled off to her quarters behind the kitchen.

"She likes him."

Antonio glanced over at her. "Really?"

"When your dad came to the house the night he and I flew to Barcelona, I saw looks pass between them. I got the distinct impression she'd called him and told him I was bored with nothing to do. Now I wonder if it isn't more than that."

"So all this time I thought my dad was a meddler, I actually have two meddlers in my life?"

She playfully swatted his arm. "You're missing the big picture. I think your head housekeeper is in love with your dad!"

He shook his head. "Poor Rosina."

"Why? Your dad is great. I think he and Rosina would make a cute couple."

"I think she's wishing on a star if she thinks that's ever going to happen."

His negativity surprised Laura Beth. When she peeked over at him, she saw something in his eyes she'd never seen before. She'd always known he was wounded. She'd believed the loss of his beloved wife had leveled him. Now she knew it was more than that. That he'd fallen out of love with his wife long before her death, when he'd lost a child. And something about this situation seemed to be bringing it all back for him.

Carefully, quietly, she said, "He wouldn't want anything to do with her because of her class? Because she's the maid?"

"Because he's in his seventies and he's never even slowed down, let alone settled down. The one woman who might have caught him with her pregnancy—with me—he summarily dismissed from his life. If she's in love with him, Rosina will get her heart broken, because my dad can't settle down."

She tried to make the connection. Was there something about Constanzo deserting Antonio's mom and the loss of Antonio's own child that connected? What could have made him so angry?

They finished their sandwiches and a hush fell over the kitchen. Her mind skipped back to the studio, to how they'd been kissing when Antonio got the call. With Constanzo in no real danger, would they pick up where they'd left off?

Antonio caught her hand. "You must be tired."

She swallowed. "Truthfully, I haven't had enough time to think about it today."

Their gazes met. He smiled and she could almost hear the question he wanted to ask. *Will you come to my room with me?* They'd been on the verge of making love and everything inside her wanted to go with him, to give herself to him, to take away his pain.

She waited for him to ask the question.

His eyes darkened as he studied her face.

The urge rose up to bridge the gap between them and kiss him. To make the first move.

But that silly shy fear of hers filled her. She needed to know—it had to be *clear* that he wanted her.

He released her fingers and pulled back. "I'll see you in the morning."

Confusion filled her. For all the times and ways he'd confided, telling her what troubled him tonight should be easy. They should be heading for his room together, talking things out, making love. Instead, he was walking away.

He stopped at the kitchen door and faced her. "With Constanzo having tests in the morning, maybe we could get in a few hours in the studio before we go to the hospital?"

The studio. She'd gotten him to tell her about his wife

in the studio. Whatever the cause of this new sadness, she could get it out of him tomorrow.

They ate breakfast quietly. Clearly believing his father was in good hands, Antonio ate toast while reading the paper. Laura Beth took slow, measured breaths. He wasn't upset this morning. But his dad had also had a heart attack the day before. Maybe the sadness she was so sure she'd seen while they'd eaten sandwiches had been nothing more than sadness over nearly losing Constanzo? Maybe she'd made a mountain out of a molehill?

She slipped away while he finished his second cup of coffee and raced upstairs to slip into the black dress and spike heels. The dining room was empty when she returned, so she headed for the studio.

She found him assembling brushes and paints and simply headed for the chaise.

"Ready?" He peeked from behind the canvas and laughed. "Ah. Not just ready, ahead of me."

She smiled, but her lips wobbled. Something about the mood in the room didn't feel right. How could he have been so utterly sad the day before and be almost happy today?

"Is that bad?"

"I like eagerness in a woman."

He was trying to sound light and flippant, but having spent so much time with him Laura Beth noticed the strain in his voice. Her fears came crashing back. As any child would, he'd been upset about his father the day before, but something else had happened.

"Could you straighten the fabric at your back? There's a kink I don't like."

She nodded and reached behind her to find the unwanted fold in her dress, but couldn't reach it.

"Here. Let me."

He walked over. As he pushed her long hair out of the way, she could feel his fingers skim across her back. She drew in a quick breath. Pinpricks of excitement danced along her flesh.

Looking over her shoulder at him, she raised her eyes to meet his and his fingers stopped as their gazes met.

"You're very beautiful."

And here it was. The real truth between them. He found her beautiful. He saw her in a way no man ever had. And it didn't just thrill her. It seemed to set her free. To turn her into the woman she wanted to be.

"You're very handsome."

His fingers moved from the fabric and traced a line up her shoulder. Warm and sure, his hand flattened on her back as the other went to her waist to turn her to him.

Neither waited for the other to move. His head came down as she rose up a bit to meet him and their lips met in a reunion of delicious passion. Wave after wave of heavenly delight flooded her as their kiss went on and on.

When she would have thought he'd move away, he caught her by the shoulders and deepened the kiss. She met his fierce kiss with her own fierceness. When he pulled back, his mouth fell to her neck, skimming wet kisses along the line of her collarbone.

She shuddered as her eyes closed in ecstasy. "I love you."

The words came out naturally, easily. Still, she wasn't surprised when he stopped kissing her. This was momentous for them. They might have been tumbling to this point for weeks, but neither had ever said the words. She opened her eyes and smiled expectantly. But instead of the sheen of passion or the warmth of love, pain filled his eyes.

He gazed at her longingly, as if she held the secrets to his happiness, but he said, "I don't love you."

For thirty seconds, her ears rang with the silence, then as the reality of what he'd said sank in, her heart exploded in her chest. An indescribable ache radiated to every part of her body. The words *I don't believe you* sprang to her tongue, but she cursed them. When would she ever learn she was Laura Beth Matthews, simple girl? Not glamour girl like Eloise or earth mother like Olivia. But plain Laura Beth Matthews, IT person who couldn't find a job, and who was never going to be loved with passion.

She pulled away from him. "I see."

"I don't think you do."

He reached for her but she shook him off. Thank God for good, old-fashioned American pride. Her chin lifted. Her thoughts cleared.

"I understand very well." She caught his gaze, working to hide the pain that sliced through her, cutting her to the core, making her feel like the world's biggest idiot. "A lot more than you think." She drew in a calming breath, telling herself she could scream or cry or whatever she wanted to do as soon as he was gone. But right now she had to get him away from her. "Go see your father."

He stepped back. Confusion clouded his dark brown eyes.

So she smiled. Though it physically hurt to force her lips upward and to hold back her tears, she managed because she refused, absolutely refused to look like a fool in front of another man. "I think we both need a little time to cool off before we get back to the painting, and your dad's going to be griping at the nurses." She studied the lines of his aristocratic face, the wild black hair, the set of his jaw. He would say she was memorizing him, and maybe she was. Because she knew this would be the last time she saw him.

The pain of that sliced through her, but she ignored it. She took another step back. "You better go rescue them."

He ran his hand along the back of his neck as if confused. "What are we doing?"

She had no idea what he was doing, but she was leaving. He was a brilliant but broken man, and she'd walked right into the trap of loving him, thinking she could help him when clearly she couldn't.

"We need a cooling-off period and you should be checking up on your dad." She lifted her chin again and smiled shakily. "I need some time."

"I'm sorry—"

She cut him off. "Don't make this any weirder than it already is. I'm fine. I misinterpreted what was going on between us." She shrugged. "It happens all the time. No big deal. I just need a break. And you going to see your dad is the best way for me to get myself together."

Antonio's heart seized at the loss of her as she stormed out of the studio, but he let her go. Because it was for her good. He was an angry, bitter man, mourning the loss not of a deceitful wife but a child. And she was a naive young pregnant woman who'd already gotten involved with the wrong man once.

He wouldn't tie her to him, but more than that, he wouldn't taint the experience of her first child with his wounds, his regrets.

CHAPTER TWELVE

LAURA BETH CALLED Bernice and within an hour Constanzo's plane was ready for her at the private airstrip. She climbed the steps. At the top she paused, taking one final look at the beautiful Italian countryside.

Bernice had tried to talk her out of leaving, but she'd explained that her mind was made up. She said goodbye to Rosina and drove herself to the airstrip, leaving Antonio's car to be picked up by staff.

Strapping herself into the plane seat, she remembered flying to Italy, eating French toast, falling asleep beside Antonio, who'd put a cover over her. Her heart lurched, but the memory of his rejection poured through her. Dear God. She'd never been so surprised. She'd been so sure he'd say he loved her too.

Straightening in her seat, she scolded herself for letting herself remember even one minute of their time together. She'd had warning after warning that he wasn't ready for what she needed. Twice he'd stepped back rather than kiss her. He hadn't wanted her to go to Barcelona. Yet she'd ignored every signal he sent because he was a wounded man, so desperately in need of love that, of course, she'd longed to love him. Handsome, talented and desperate for love, he'd been just a little too much to resist.

Pain threatened to overwhelm her, but she shoved it down. She had responsibilities and realities of her own, and she'd come to her senses. After one quick pass of her hand over her tummy, she snuggled into a blanket, intending to fall asleep. But tears welled in her eyes. Her chest heaved. And sobs overtook her.

Alone on a plane with no one to see or hear her, she gave in and let herself weep.

On the ground in Kentucky, she rented a car. When she used her check card to pay for it, she discovered she didn't merely have the full salary Constanzo had promised her, but Antonio's father had also ponied up the promised severance pay.

She called Bernice to have it taken back, but Bernice laughed. "Are you kidding? Constanzo is happy to be alive. He's so generous right now that I'm surprised he didn't double it. He'll never take it back. Besides, he gave orders for the money to be given to you weeks ago, when you first arrived. No matter when you left that money was going to you...so it's yours."

Though Constanzo's generosity was a bit overboard, Laura Beth understood that he felt he owed her. Helping her set up her new life was probably how he'd deal with her leaving. He needed to know she'd be okay and money was his tool. So maybe it would be best to just take what he offered. She'd fulfilled at least part of her duties to Constanzo by helping Antonio clear out his office and getting him to a gallery opening. She'd also gotten him painting again—Constanzo's real goal. So, yeah. She could understand why Constanzo had been so generous.

Plus, the money meant she could move on. Never see Antonio again.

That filled her heart with pain. She let herself feel

it as a reminder that she never wanted to be so foolish again, but she didn't really need a reminder. In her
heart, she knew she'd never love another man the way
she loved Antonio.

She arrived at her parents' house a little before dawn.
She made coffee and pancakes, and, as she expected,
the scents woke her mom and dad and her two brothers.

As hugs were exchanged, she swallowed hard. She
didn't want to ruin this reunion, but she knew it was
time to accept her fate and do what needed to be done.

When everyone had a few pancakes on their plates,
she smiled at the group. "I have some news."

Her tall, strapping construction worker dad laughed,
and said, "You're staying in Italy," as if it were a fore-
gone conclusion.

She shook her head. "No. No more Italy. I'm actually
home for good. I got a huge severance from the gentleman who'd hired me. I can afford to buy a house here."

Her mom clutched her chest. "You're back?"

She nodded. "For good."

Then her mom surprised her. "Oh, sweetie, we love
you and we love the idea of you living in town with
us—" she caught Laura Beth's gaze "—but you wanted
so much more for yourself. A big-time career. Are you
going to be happy here?"

Laura Beth swallowed as unhappiness swelled in her.
Still, it wasn't the big-time career she would miss. It was
Antonio. The real love of her life. But how could she
explain that to her parents when she was pregnant with
another man's child? Worse, how could she explain that
when Antonio didn't feel for her what she felt her him?

She couldn't. Her love for Antonio would have to
stay her hidden secret. Another cross to bear.

For her parents' sake, she brightened when she said,

"Yes, I'll be very happy here, because I have a child to raise."

At her parents' confused look, she said, "I'm pregnant. Bruce doesn't want to marry me, but I'm okay with that. I don't love him either." An arrow pierced her heart again when she thought of the man she did love, but she ignored it. "And with the severance pay I got from Mr. Bartulocci, I can buy a house and support myself until after the baby's born. Then I may need to take some courses, like accounting, so I can find a job around here." She squeezed her mom's hand. "But it's all good."

Nothing was good. Antonio glanced around the private suite they'd given his dad, at the rows and rows of flowers that covered every flat surface in the room, and even parts of the floor. Still, his father grumbled.

"It's hot in here."

"It's almost June. It's supposed to be hot."

"I want to see Laura Beth."

Pain squeezed Antonio's heart, but he forced himself not to show it. When he'd returned to the house the day before, her room had been empty. Rosina knew nothing, though her crying suggested otherwise. He'd had to call Bernice before he got the news that she'd taken the plane and gone to Kentucky.

"She went home."

Constanzo kicked his covers around, trying to get comfortable, but obviously failing. "I can't believe she went home. What did you say? What did you do?"

"Interesting how you assume I somehow drove her off."

"Didn't you?"

He had. He knew he had. But this was none of his father's business. Plus, there were bigger issues in Laura Beth's life than a heartbreak from a guy who hadn't deserved her love.

He sucked in a breath and faced his father. "She's pregnant."

Constanzo stopped struggling. "Oh, my God! How did I raise you to let the mother of your child go? Did you learn nothing from my mistakes?"

Antonio shook his head. "It's not my baby."

Constanzo's eyes narrowed. "Is this why she was so eager to come to Italy?"

Antonio nodded. "She needed some time to think things through and a place she could gather herself while she figured out what to do. You provided it."

"I am good that way."

Oh, how the man could turn anything to his favor! "You're a crabby old man."

"I anticipate!" Constanzo yelled, then he sucked in a long, slow breath. Antonio tensed, worried something was wrong, but Constanzo quietly said, "You are going to make me pay until the end of time, aren't you?"

Confused, Antonio caught his father's gaze. "What? What am I making you pay for this time?"

"Leaving you." He brushed his hand in dismissal. "No. That is not correct. You aren't making me pay for leaving you. You are making me pay for everything wrong that happened in your life after your mother died."

Antonio bristled. He did nothing but ask, "How high?" when his dad said, "Jump." He catered to his whims and wishes. Canceled plans. Made plans. How could Constanzo even hint that Antonio was somehow making him pay?

"That's insanity."

"Is it? You always hold yourself away. You love me but you won't give me love."

Antonio gaped at him. "Are you lying in a hospital bed, recovering from a heart attack, splitting hairs with me?"

Constanzo fussed with the covers. "Yes."

"You have got to be kidding me."

"I almost died. It gives a man clarity."

"Right."

"I am right! I want my son to love me and respect me. Not give me bits and pieces of affection."

"Maybe you should have thought of that before you kicked my mom out of your office."

"And there we have it."

Antonio shook his head and turned away from his dad. "I'm not having this conversation. I'm tired, I'm stressed and you're pushing me into saying things I don't mean."

"And why are you stressed? I'm the one who almost died."

Antonio tossed his hands in disgust. "There's no winning with you."

"There could be. All you have to do is love me like a dad, not like an enemy you're forced to interact with." When Antonio said nothing, he sighed. "Forgive me for not believing your mom."

Antonio squeezed his eyes shut.

"Then forgive Gisella for being a slut."

His eyes popped open and he spun to face his dad. "What?"

Constanzo laughed. "You think I don't know? You think my own daughter-in-law could flaunt her affairs in my favorite cities and word would not get back to me?"

Antonio rubbed his hand down his face.

"You carry the weight of betrayal like a good-luck charm. Something you're afraid to set down for fear if you do bad luck will return. Because I didn't trust your mom, you're afraid to trust me. And because Gisella humiliated you, you won't trust Laura Beth."

"If it were that simple, I think I could get beyond it."

"Then tell me the part that's complicated."

He blew out a breath. "Gisella aborted our child."

His dad blinked. "Oh."

"And Laura Beth is pregnant. I have mourned the loss of my child for two long years. I wake up most days knowing I should have a son or daughter playing in my yard. I cannot handle having a pregnant woman under my roof, and it isn't fair to subject her to my anger when she's not at fault."

Constanzo closed his eyes and shook his head. "I am so sorry."

"Why? It's not like you understand. You very easily let my mother go…then forgot her. Forgot *me*. How could you possibly understand my loss?"

"I think it's time I tell you what really happened with your mom."

Antonio slowly lifted his gaze to meet his dad's. "I'm not in the mood, Dad."

"But this is finally the right time. The only time. If you don't change now, I fear you will be gone for good."

Gobsmacked, he only stared at his dad. "*I* need to change?"

"Yes. Just listen." Constanzo cleared his throat and quietly said, "Your mother was a rebound relationship."

Antonio frowned. "I thought you'd been dating?"

"We had. I'd lost the love of my life and one day your mother happened to be at a club where I was socializing. We struck up a conversation. One thing led to another and she came home with me."

Antonio shook his head, not sure how the hell this was supposed to help him. "She was a one-night stand?"

"She was a rebound. I'd been ridiculously in love with a woman I thought loved me too. But she hadn't. She hadn't been with me for my money or for love. A rich heiress, she was simply biding time. Waiting for a better guy to come around."

"So you did the same thing with my mom."

He winced. "Yes. And after a few weeks, I let her go." He fussed with the covers. "Then a few weeks after that she came to me with the pregnancy story and I thought it was a ruse. A way to get back with me or get back at me."

"So you kicked her out of your office and forgot her because you were busy?"

Constanzo nodded. "And though it seemed like the right thing at the time, ten years later I suddenly realized what I'd done. If she really had been pregnant, I'd tossed away a child."

Antonio sniffed a laugh.

"Oh, you think you're so superior. But my loss of you is not so much different than the loss of your child. Except in my case I had a hand in things. But when a person comes to his senses and realizes he's thrown away his one chance at real happiness..." He paused, caught Antonio's gaze. "It more than hurts. Sometimes, it stops a life."

Antonio swallowed hard.

"Did you love Gisella?"

"At one time."

"But the love died?"

He glanced up at his dad. "I'm not sure she had any love for me to die."

"So you feel a fool?"

He drew in a long breath and expelled it quickly. "That sort of gets lost in the grief I feel over my child."

"And you don't see the second chance you've been handed?"

He frowned.

"You love Laura Beth."

He shook his head. "She's a very nice woman. Far too good to be dragged into my pit."

"Oh, pit, schmit."

"Excuse me?"

"Now you are splitting hairs. Maybe because you're afraid."

"Afraid? Hell, yes, I'm afraid. How do I know I won't see my baby every time I look at hers? How do I know I can be a good husband when the only chance I got to try resulted in failure?"

"Do you love Laura Beth?"

He squeezed his eyes shut. "I have feelings for her that are beyond expression. Sometimes when she's around it's comfortable. Other days, she makes me think. I can't imagine anyplace I'd go, anything I'd do that wouldn't be more fun if she was there."

Constanzo laughed. "Oh, my son. You have it bad and it scares you."

Antonio licked his suddenly dry lips. "I failed with a woman who seemed to be tailor-made for me—"

"Men like you and me, Antonio, we're not made for princesses or supermodels. We're high maintenance ourselves."

Antonio laughed.

"We are made for the Laura Beths of the world. The

women who bring sunshine. The women who make us stop and enjoy life. If you let her go, you will regret it for the rest of your days. But more than that, if you can't finally learn to forgive, the regret you have over her leaving will be nothing compared to the sadness you will find when you wake up one day and discover you created your own prison."

Antonio looked over at his dad. "You want me to forgive you?"

"For real this time. And I want you to forgive Gisella."

He sniffed a laugh. "She doesn't need my forgiveness."

Constanzo shook his head sadly. "No. But your tired soul needs the rest forgiving will give you." He patted the bed, asking for Antonio's hand. Antonio slid his hand over to his dad, who caught it and squeezed. "You lost a family, but Laura Beth is offering you another. Sometimes fate is weird like that. It cannot give you back what you lost, but sometimes it finds a replacement."

The room was quiet for a second, then Constanzo said, "If you don't take this chance, another might come along. Fate is generous. But do you want to lose Laura Beth? The real love of your life? Now that you've met her, everyone will pale compared to her. You might find happiness. But you will never again find this joy."

Antonio rose. He walked to the head of the bed, reached down and hugged his father. "I forgive you, you old coot."

Constanzo patted his back. "For real this time?"

He sucked in a breath. "For real this time."

"Thank you. Now, go get Laura Beth. I want the sound of small feet in our big houses."

* * *

Antonio drove his Lamborghini back home. He understood what his father was saying about his mom. He also felt a swell of regret for withholding forgiveness from his father. But going to get Laura Beth?

Even though he knew in his heart she was the one true love of his life, going to her with his heart in his hand was risky. He wasn't just afraid. He was unworthy. Despite his ability to forgive his dad, he couldn't trust. He didn't want to trust.

Too wired to do anything, he headed for his studio. He unlocked the old wooden door and went to the back room.

There on the easel was Laura Beth.

He hesitated as he walked to the pencil drawing that would become a painting. Her laughing eyes beckoned. He ran his finger down the line of her cheek. The problem wasn't fear that she'd hurt him as Gisella had. The problem was he feared she'd hurt him worse. What he felt for her went beyond the surface, beyond a desire for her beauty. He loved her in a way he never could have loved Gisella. With his whole heart and soul. And that's why he feared her.

Gisella could never have held that kind of power over him, which was why it was suddenly easy to forgive her.

Feeling free for the first time in years, he made his way back to the house and stepped into quiet. The kind of quiet that became an early grave if a man wasn't careful.

He walked upstairs, to his room, letting himself imagine the sounds of a child, a soothing lullaby from Laura Beth, the click of computer keys as he arranged for something totally American—a Disney vacation—and he laughed.

Maybe his dad was right? Maybe fate was giving him a second chance, with a different child. His child might be gone, but Laura Beth's baby needed a daddy.

His life would be so different with her. Noisy. Complicated. Rich.

All he had to do was get on his father's jet and find her.

Laura Beth dragged her mother to the fourth real estate appointment in as many days.

"There's no sidewalk," her mother groused. "I'm not coming to visit you if I'm going to get mud on my shoes every time I walk to your back door." She stopped, crossed her arms on her chest stubbornly. "Take pictures with that fancy phone of yours. I'll be in the car."

"Mom!" Laura Beth called after her mother, who strode back to the little blue car Laura Beth had bought the day before.

"You don't need me for this one," her mom yelled back as she opened the car door and slipped inside. "I've got a key. I'll listen to the radio and be fine."

Laura Beth sighed and turned to walk to the back door of the brand-new house. Of course it didn't have sidewalks. The contractor hadn't poured them yet. And since when was her mom so picky? For Pete's sake. She'd eagerly seen the other three houses, but it had been like wrestling a bear to get her to come with her to see this house, and when push came to shove she wouldn't even go inside.

Whatever. She was an adult now. Able to make a decision about a house without her mommy.

She marched to the back door, pushed it open and called, "Hello? Anybody here?" It was a stupid question, since the Realtor's red Cadillac was in the driveway. Of course, he was here.

Still, before she could call again, the kitchen caught her attention. Happy green wood cabinets with creamy granite countertops filled a huge room that spilled out into a family room section. She let her purse slide to the floor and walked a little farther inside. She could put a table in the area with the bay window that would let in the morning sun, and decorate the family room area with sturdy furniture to accommodate her baby.

Her baby.

Her heart fluttered a bit. In the past four days of refusing to think about Antonio, she'd spent a lot of time wondering about her baby, thinking about whether it was a boy or girl, knowing she had to get a house set up before he or she was born.

"Hello?" she called again, heading for the big formal dining room. Seeing the high ceilings, she immediately pictured Antonio painting. Not green walls or white trim. But a mural. He'd love this space.

Pain pinged through her and she shook her head, reminding herself she wasn't allowed to think about him.

"Hello?" She walked out of the dining room and into a living room with a huge stone fireplace. Her first thought was of Antonio insisting they buy some kind of funky furniture for the room, or maybe artifacts from a dig in Mongolia. She laughed and this time reminded herself more sternly that she wasn't allowed to think about him. But that only caused her to realize the reason she kept thinking about him was that the house was probably out of her price range. Constanzo had been generous, but he wasn't an idiot. He hadn't given her enough to buy a mansion. And though Tucker had called and offered her a job, she fully intended to be wise with her money and not overspend.

As she walked up the sweeping stairway to the second floor, she knew beyond a shadow of a doubt that she couldn't afford this house. Searching for the real estate agent, she knew she had to tell him that she didn't want it. The place was huge. The master bedroom alone could fit two of the New York City apartment she'd shared with Eloise and Olivia.

She ambled into the bathroom, which had brown tiles, a travertine floor and a double-sink vanity.

"Hey."

She spun around. Expecting to see her Realtor, she gasped when she saw Antonio standing in front of the open stone shower. Because he was the last person she expected to see on the outskirts of tiny Starlight, Kentucky, she opened her mouth to ask him what he was doing there, but no words came out.

He looked crazy amazing. His hair was a mess, the way it was after a day of painting, her favorite time with him—which made her wonder if she was having some kind of sadness-related hallucination.

"What are you doing here?"

The best way to end a hallucination would be to force it to talk. If he said something impossible—like that he loved her—she would know she was imagining things.

"I heard you're in the market for a house."

Now, that was an illusion if she ever heard one. Her Antonio didn't talk about commonsense, normal stuff. Still, she answered, "Yes."

"Do you like this one?"

She laughed and glanced around. "Jeez, who wouldn't? Everything is gorgeous, but I think it's too big."

He pushed off the shower wall. "Of course it's big. You're looking at it because you're thinking down the line to when you have more kids. Anticipating, like Constanzo."

She laughed out loud. Good Lord, her imagination was powerful. "I'm going to have trouble enough raising one child."

"Your mother will help."

She sucked in a breath. "I know."

He stepped toward her. "I will help."

"Okay, time to end this hallucination."

He laughed. "I wondered why you were so calm. You think I'm a figment of your imagination?"

She winced and squeezed her eyes shut. Her time with him had seemed like a dream. The four days since she'd been here in Starlight she'd sort of vibrated with confusion. Was it any wonder she was having trouble with reality?

"Okay. I'm an idiot." Her eyes popped open. "What are you doing here?"

"Constanzo forced me to talk about our relationship and to forgive him."

"Oh."

"Weird, huh?"

Not half as weird as having the love of her life in the bathroom of the house she was looking at. Tears filled her eyes as she took in his handsome face. He was everything she'd ever wanted. Even things she didn't realize she wanted. But he didn't love her. He'd said it. And by damn, she wanted to be loved.

Passionately.

Men who told you they didn't love you did not fit that bill.

She took a step back, away from him. "So what does Constanzo forcing you to forgive him have to do with you being here?"

"I looked at your Realtor's offerings and I decided this is the best house for us."

Her heart stuttered, but absolutely positive she hadn't heard correctly, she said, "For us?"

"I've done some thinking in the past few days." He walked around the big bathroom. "And my dad forced me to do even more thinking. He made me realize my problem was that I couldn't trust anyone."

She bristled. She already knew that and so did he. So what the hell was he doing talking about a house for *them*? "Are you saying you don't trust me?"

"I thought I couldn't trust anyone. You could have been the woman in the moon and I would have held myself back." He caught her gaze. "I'm sorry about that, by the way."

She sniffed. "Right."

"I am."

"So you're asking me to accept second-best? You want us to live in this house together, but only if I can accept that you'll never trust me? Wow. You're a piece of work."

He laughed, but walked closer and stopped in front of her. "I'm not a piece of work." He tapped her nose. "And if you don't let me finish this in my own way, nothing's ever going to be right between us."

She frowned. But he put a finger over her lips to silence her. "I'm not asking you to live with me. I'm not saying that I don't trust you. I do trust you. I think I have for a while. It took weeks for me to tell you my story, but eventually you got the whole thing out of me."

Her heart lifted, but she couldn't let herself dare to believe. He'd hurt her because she allowed herself to fantasize that he might love her. She would not let him hurt her again. "I think the truth is you don't trust yourself."

He shrugged. "Maybe. You have to admit it takes a pretty stupid guy to marry a supermodel and not realize she's using him."

Because he said it lightly, she almost laughed, but this conversation was too important. "You loved her."

"Yeah. I did."

Her heart felt the pinch of that. This man had been married to the woman dubbed the most beautiful woman in the world three times. Laura Beth knew Gisella hadn't been as pure of heart as the rest of the world believed, but that couldn't take away from her beauty. How could Laura Beth ever think a man like Antonio would consider *her* beautiful?

"But, Laura Beth, I love you more."

Her head snapped up. "You do?"

"Yes." He ran his finger along the line of her jaw. "You are sweet and fun and funny. You are also beautiful. So beautiful that my memories of silly women like Gisella disappear."

Her breath caught. "You don't have to say things like that."

"I say only what's true." He slid his hands to her waist. "Now, will you live with me in this house?"

Her breath shivered. Live with him? In Starlight, Kentucky? Where her mom and all her friends would see that he liked her enough to live with her but not to marry her?

She stepped back. "No."

He blinked. "No?"

"I know you're scarred. I know it took moving mountains for you to trust." Her chin lifted. "But I deserve better than living with you."

He laughed. "Oh, that is all?"

She took another few steps back. "Don't belittle what I want." Her chin lifted even higher. "What I need."

He shook his head and removed a ring box from his back pocket. "I did this all wrong. I'm sorry." He opened the box to reveal a stunning diamond. "Will you marry me?"

She pressed her trembling lips together, met his gaze.

"You are my heart and soul. You are what I've been searching for forever. My father thought things between him and me were awkward because I couldn't forgive him. The truth was our relationship was awkward because it wasn't what I was searching for. Yes, I need him in my life. But what I really wanted was love. A true love. You are that love."

Tears filled her eyes. "Oh, Antonio." She fell into his arms.

And he breathed a sigh of relief. In those seconds with her arms around him and her body pressed against his, he felt his soul knit together. He felt his mother smiling down on him from heaven. He could see the family he and Laura Beth would create and that his place in the world wouldn't be secured because he was a great artist, but because he would be a part of something bigger than himself. A family.

And he could see his dad reveling in that.

EPILOGUE

ANTONIO AND LAURA Beth waited until baby Isabella was six months old before they had their wedding. With a huge white tent in the yard of Constanzo's country home, the old billionaire about burst with pride as he greeted guests, Rosina at his side. Not as Antonio's housekeeper or even a family friend. But as his fiancé.

Laura Beth watched from the second-floor window of the room she, Olivia and Eloise used to dress for the wedding.

"He is a crazy old man."

Pinning her veil into Laura Beth's fancy updo, Olivia laughed. "He might be crazy, but he brought at least two of us together with our perfect mates."

"So maybe he's wise," Eloise said from her position kneeling between Laura Beth and a centuries-old vanity said to have been used by Marie Antoinette, as she straightened Laura Beth's train. Eloise's boss, Artie Best, had designed the pale peach bridesmaids' dresses. But Eloise herself had created Laura Beth's gown.

With her hair up and her dress fastened, Laura Beth turned to look at herself in the full-length mirror. Strapless, her dress rode her curves and flared out a few inches below her hips to become a frothy skirt with lace trim. Sequins sparkled everywhere, including in the veil that flowed gracefully from her hair along her shoulders and to the floor.

Tears filled her eyes.

Eloise clutched her chest. "You don't like it?"

"I told you in all three fittings that I love it."

Olivia said, "Then what's wrong?"

Laura Beth faced her friends. "I'm beautiful."

As Eloise collapsed with relief, Olivia hugged Laura Beth. "Of course you are. Now let's get downstairs before Isabella starts crying for her mom."

The ceremony was a quiet but loving affair. Antonio looked amazing in his black tux, with her friends' husbands as his groomsmen. The sun shone down on the white tent filled with happy friends.

Just as the minister pronounced them man and wife, Isabella began to cry and Laura Beth took her from her mother, then Antonio took her from Laura Beth. She, Antonio and Isabella walked down the aisle to the sound of Constanzo sobbing loudly.

With joy.

They hoped.

As they greeted their guests, she watched Constanzo cast a quick look to heaven. Obviously believing no one saw or heard, he quietly said, "See, *carissima*. I finally did right by our boy."

Her eyes filled with tears, but she totally understood.

* * * * *

MILLS & BOON®
Hardback – February 2015

ROMANCE

The Redemption of Darius Sterne	Carole Mortimer
The Sultan's Harem Bride	Annie West
Playing by the Greek's Rules	Sarah Morgan
Innocent in His Diamonds	Maya Blake
To Wear His Ring Again	Chantelle Shaw
The Man to Be Reckoned With	Tara Pammi
Claimed by the Sheikh	Rachael Thomas
Delucca's Marriage Contract	Abby Green
Her Brooding Italian Boss	Susan Meier
The Heiress's Secret Baby	Jessica Gilmore
A Pregnancy, a Party & a Proposal	Teresa Carpenter
Best Friend to Wife and Mother?	Caroline Anderson
The Sheikh Doctor's Bride	Meredith Webber
A Baby to Heal Their Hearts	Kate Hardy
One Hot Desert Night	Kristi Gold
Snowed In with Her Ex	Andrea Laurence
Cowgirls Don't Cry	Silver James
Terms of a Texas Marriage	Lauren Canan

MEDICAL

A Date with Her Valentine Doc	Melanie Milburne
It Happened in Paris...	Robin Gianna
Temptation in Paradise	Joanna Neil
The Surgeon's Baby Secret	Amber McKenzie

0115 GEN STD HB

MILLS & BOON®
Large Print – February 2015

ROMANCE

An Heiress for His Empire	Lucy Monroe
His for a Price	Caitlin Crews
Commanded by the Sheikh	Kate Hewitt
The Valquez Bride	Melanie Milburne
The Uncompromising Italian	Cathy Williams
Prince Hafiz's Only Vice	Susanna Carr
A Deal Before the Altar	Rachael Thomas
The Billionaire in Disguise	Soraya Lane
The Unexpected Honeymoon	Barbara Wallace
A Princess by Christmas	Jennifer Faye
His Reluctant Cinderella	Jessica Gilmore

HISTORICAL

Zachary Black: Duke of Debauchery	Carole Mortimer
The Truth About Lady Felkirk	Christine Merrill
The Courtesan's Book of Secrets	Georgie Lee
Betrayed by His Kiss	Amanda McCabe
Falling for Her Captor	Elisabeth Hobbes

MEDICAL

Tempted by Her Boss	Scarlet Wilson
His Girl From Nowhere	Tina Beckett
Falling For Dr Dimitriou	Anne Fraser
Return of Dr Irresistible	Amalie Berlin
Daring to Date Her Boss	Joanna Neil
A Doctor to Heal Her Heart	Annie Claydon

MILLS & BOON®
Hardback – March 2015

ROMANCE

The Taming of Xander Sterne	Carole Mortimer
In the Brazilian's Debt	Susan Stephens
At the Count's Bidding	Caitlin Crews
The Sheikh's Sinful Seduction	Dani Collins
The Real Romero	Cathy Williams
His Defiant Desert Queen	Jane Porter
Prince Nadir's Secret Heir	Michelle Conder
Princess's Secret Baby	Carol Marinelli
The Renegade Billionaire	Rebecca Winters
The Playboy of Rome	Jennifer Faye
Reunited with Her Italian Ex	Lucy Gordon
Her Knight in the Outback	Nikki Logan
Baby Twins to Bind Them	Carol Marinelli
The Firefighter to Heal Her Heart	Annie O'Neil
Thirty Days to Win His Wife	Andrea Laurence
Her Forbidden Cowboy	Charlene Sands
The Blackstone Heir	Dani Wade
After Hours with Her Ex	Maureen Child

MEDICAL

Tortured by Her Touch	Dianne Drake
It Happened in Vegas	Amy Ruttan
The Family She Needs	Sue MacKay
A Father for Poppy	Abigail Gordon

MILLS & BOON®
Large Print – March 2015

ROMANCE

A Virgin for His Prize	Lucy Monroe
The Valquez Seduction	Melanie Milburne
Protecting the Desert Princess	Carol Marinelli
One Night with Morelli	Kim Lawrence
To Defy a Sheikh	Maisey Yates
The Russian's Acquisition	Dani Collins
The True King of Dahaar	Tara Pammi
The Twelve Dates of Christmas	Susan Meier
At the Chateau for Christmas	Rebecca Winters
A Very Special Holiday Gift	Barbara Hannay
A New Year Marriage Proposal	Kate Hardy

HISTORICAL

Darian Hunter: Duke of Desire	Carole Mortimer
Rescued by the Viscount	Anne Herries
The Rake's Bargain	Lucy Ashford
Unlaced by Candlelight	Various
The Warrior's Winter Bride	Denise Lynn

MEDICAL

A Secret Shared...	Marion Lennox
Flirting with the Doc of Her Dreams	Janice Lynn
The Doctor Who Made Her Love Again	Susan Carlisle
The Maverick Who Ruled Her Heart	Susan Carlisle
After One Forbidden Night...	Amber McKenzie
Dr Perfect on Her Doorstep	Lucy Clark

MILLS & BOON®

Why shop at millsandboon.co.uk?

Each year, thousands of romance readers find their perfect read at millsandboon.co.uk. That's because we're passionate about bringing you the very best romantic fiction. Here are some of the advantages of shopping at www.millsandboon.co.uk:

* **Get new books first**—you'll be able to buy your favourite books one month before they hit the shops

* **Get exclusive discounts**—you'll also be able to buy our specially created monthly collections, with up to 50% off the RRP

* **Find your favourite authors**—latest news, interviews and new releases for all your favourite authors and series on our website, plus ideas for what to try next

* **Join in**—once you've bought your favourite books, don't forget to register with us to rate, review and join in the discussions

Visit **www.millsandboon.co.uk**
for all this and more today!